THE HUNTER MAIDEN

FEMINIST FOLKTALES FROM AROUND THE WORLD | Vol. IV

THE HUNTER MAIDEN

FEMINIST FOLKTALES FROM AROUND THE WORLD | Vol. IV

ETHEL JOHNSTON PHELPS

Introduction by RENÉE WATSON | With illustrations by SUKI BOYNTON

FP

FEMINIST PRESS
AT THE CITY UNIVERSITY
OF NEW YORK
NEW YORK CITY

Published in 2017 by the Feminist Press
at the City University of New York
The Graduate Center
365 Fifth Avenue, Suite 5406
New York, NY 10016

feministpress.org

First Feminist Press edition 2017

This book was made possible thanks to a grant from New York State Council on the Arts with the support of Governor Andrew Cuomo and the New York State Legislature.

First printing October 2017

Cover and text design by Suki Boynton

Library of Congress Cataloging-in-Publication Data is available for this title.

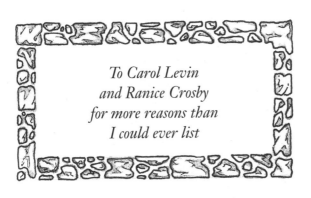

*To Carol Levin
and Ranice Crosby
for more reasons than
I could ever list*

CONTENTS

INTRODUCTION
RENÉE WATSON

We cannot create what we can't imagine.
　　　　　　　　　—LUCILLE CLIFTON

Let's imagine a world where women are seen as whole beings and not as body parts, quests to be conquered, or damsels to be rescued. Let's imagine a world where women save their own days, save the world, even.

Let's imagine women as hunters.

I have always been drawn to female characters who chase, pursue, explore, interrogate, rescue. Kill, even. Every good story has a character who desperately wants something. But too often the desires of female characters revolve around clichés—gaining the affection of a man or wanting to be popular at almost any cost.

But not here. This is a collection of tales that have imagined worlds where women are on the hunt, where women are in search of their own independence, of finding what will truly quench their physical, spiritual, and emotional hunger. These are women who will sacrifice and risk all for who and what they love, what they need, what they want. They are wise and they are strong. They are like the women I know in my real life who are often criticized, undervalued, silenced, or invisible.

Here, in these pages, a space has been created for their stories to be told. I believe we so desperately need these kinds of spaces—books, classrooms, writing workshops, community centers, homes—where women from all backgrounds can be seen and heard. These imaginary and actual spaces influence each other. If reality is flawed with sexist stereotypes and expectations, I should be able to read a story, a poem, and see what the world could be when characters prove to be more than those assumptions. When literature fails to show the myriad of experiences of what it means to *act like a girl*, I should be able to look in my world and find many examples of girls and women living life on their own terms. What we experience, what we imagine, and what we create are always in conversation with each other.

This collection is a space where that conversation lives. Some of these women I feel like I've met before. Some of them have traits I recognize in myself. Others feel so outside of what I am used to, what I know. They all have a place here, and because they do, they can influence and impact what is created and imagined about women.

Here, Mulha, a fourteen-year-old South African girl, comes face-to-face with a monster and does not "waste time crying." She does not crumble under adversity but instead finds light even in the darkest of circumstances. The thing that should destroy her becomes a means of provision. Mulha's story reminds me of the women who raised me, who made a way out of no way, who found joy when all there seemed to be around them was pain and sorrow. There is a space for them here. Mulha's story validates the years of waiting on an answer to a prayer, on the sweet redemption that comes after years of being forgotten and overlooked.

In these pages, Elsa in "Elsa and the Evil Wizard" makes space for women determined to stand on their own two feet. Elsa refuses to be wooed by an arrogant suitor who only values her physical beauty and has no interest in who she really is. What I love about Elsa, and women like her, is her willingness to take a stand not just for herself but also for all types of women who deserve to be seen. Elsa uses her smarts to rescue herself, yes, but then she goes beyond self-preservation and devises a plan so that no other girl is preyed upon by this evil wizard.

In the tale of "The Husband Who Stayed Home," we meet a brilliant wife who switches roles with her husband, proving she can do everything he does and not only be good at it, but can also rescue him from the disaster he creates when he tries to take care of her responsibilities. She is not shy about her capabilities. She isn't self-deprecating and doesn't downplay the fact that she can do many things well. Once she is out of the box, she refuses to be put back in. She has outgrown its boundaries.

In the Zuni tale, "The Hunter Maiden," we meet a girl who has the bold belief that there is no reason why she shouldn't be able to hunt. Her brothers are dead and her father is too feeble. There is no other option for this girl—if her family doesn't eat, her family will starve, die. The stakes are too high for her to stay in a girl's place and play by the rules. She must do "the dangerous thing." She has to.

And so do we.

In our real lives—whether writer or reader, scholar or student—we must do the dangerous things: challenge oppressive systems, take risks to go after the thing that will feed us, nurture us. We must provide spaces for diverse stories to be told and heard. The exchange of stories reminds us of each other's humanity. The imagined story gives us an opportunity to create a new world.

This collection has brought together a diverse cast of women who, individually, are remarkable and intriguing. Together, they are powerful. There is strength in this collection. There are no easy solutions for our heroines; there are no princes who come to make everything better with just one kiss. These stories tell girls it is okay to be afraid, to be flawed, to be hungry, to be curious, to be angry. These are complex characters who are perfectly imperfect, who don't need fixing, per se, but rather a space to exist *as is*. Imagine it.

In some ways, *The Hunter Maiden* reminds me of the gatherings I often have with friends—sometimes brunch or sometimes a meet up at home. We gather, all of us so different from each other, all of us bringing our stories of loving, parenting, creating, living, womaning to the group. It is there, in that place, during the exchange of stories, that we bear witness to each other, that we heal, that we question, that we imagine the world we want to create.

I am thankful for those women. I am thankful for this collection. Both provide a space for women to *be*.

PREFACE
ETHEL JOHNSTON PHELPS

The traditional fairy and folktales in this collection, as in my earlier books of tales, have one characteristic in common: they all portray spirited, courageous heroines. Although a great number of such collections are in print, this type of heroine is surprisingly rare.

Taken as a whole, the body of traditional fairy and folktales (the two terms have become almost interchangeable) is very heavily weighted with heroes, and most of the "heroines" we do encounter are far from heroic. Always endowed with beauty—and it often appears that beauty is their only reason for being in the tale—they conform in many ways to the sentimental ideal of women in the nineteenth century. They are good, obedient, meek, submissive to authority, and naturally inferior to the heroes. They sometimes suffer cruelties but are patient under ill treatment. In most cases they are docile or helpless when confronted with danger or a difficult situation.

In short, as heroines, they do not inspire or delight, but tend to bore the reader. I think it is their meekness that repels. They are acted upon by people or events in the tale; they rarely initiate their own action to change matters. (In contrast to this type of heroine, when clever or strong women appear in folktales, they are usually portrayed as unpleasant, if not evil, characters—cruel witches, jealous stepmothers, or old hags.) It is not my intention to delve into the psychological or social meanings behind the various images of heroines in folktales, but simply to note that the vast majority are not particularly satisfying to readers today.

In actual fact, the women of much earlier centuries, particularly rural women, were strong, capable, and resourceful in positive ways as hard-working members of a family or as widows on their own. Few folktales reflect these qualities. Inevitably the question arises: How many, if any, folktales of strong, capable heroines exist in the printed sources available?

In a sense, this book grew out of that question. Over a period of three years, I read thousands of fairy and folktales in a search for tales of clever, resourceful heroines; tales in which equally courageous heroines and heroes cooperated in their adventures; tales of likeable heroines who had the spirit to take action; tales that were, in themselves, strong or appealing.

As a result of that search, the heroines in this book are quite different from the usual fairy and folktale heroines. In a few of the tales, the girls and women possess the power (or knowledge) of magic, which they use to rescue the heroes from disaster. The hero may be more physically active in the story, but he needs the powers of the self-reliant, independent heroine to save him.

In the majority of the tales, the heroines are resourceful girls and women who take action to solve a problem posed by the plot. Often they use cleverness or shrewd common sense.

All the heroines have self-confidence and a clear sense of their own worth. They possess courage, moral or physical; they do not meekly accept but seek to solve the dilemmas they face. The majority have leading roles in the story. The few who have minor roles (in terms of space) play a crucial part in the story and have an independent strength that is characteristic of all the heroines here.

Although most of the printed sources for the tales I've chosen are from the nineteenth century, the tales themselves are part of an oral, primarily rural tradition of storytelling that stretches far back in time. Each generation shaped the tales according to the values of the time, adding or subtracting details according to the teller's own sense of story. While the characters and basic story remained the same, it was this personal shaping of the tales that may explain the many variations of each story that now exist. As every folktale reader knows, different versions of the tales are found in different countries and even different continents. Variants of Cinderella and of tales of hero/heroines bewitched into nonhuman form are particularly widespread.

In giving the older tales of our heritage a fresh retelling for this generation of readers, I have exercised the traditional storyteller's privilege. I have shaped each tale, sometimes adding or omitting details, to reflect my sense of what makes it a satisfying tale. The stories "Maria Morevna" and "Finn Magic," for example, have been compressed to make a smoother flow of narrative.

Most of the tales in this book follow the story outlines of earlier sources quite closely. In a few cases I've added my own details to amplify the story's ending, as in "The Husband Who Stayed at Home" and "Elsa and the Evil Wizard."

For the tale "Lanval and the Lady Triamor," I

have used as sources the versions of fourteenth-century literary storytellers who drew on oral folktales of their period. As might be expected, this is more complex than other tales in the collection. However, there are tales to appeal to the very young as well as the more sophisticated reader. Through the tales' diversity, the reader becomes aware of the extraordinary vitality of the fairy and folktale heritage, not only in the range of imaginative fantasy but also in humor. I confess a partiality for the lighthearted tale. The humor here is most obvious in the comic tales of "Duffy and the Devil" and "The Husband Who Stayed at Home."

Two of the tales in the book deserve longer comment. The tale of Lanval dates back to the twelfth century, if not earlier, and has many variants. Fairy women who marry or mate with humans are found frequently in Celtic folktales. They are powerful, independent women who confer benefits on the man of their choice. The terms they state for the union always contain a taboo, and they always glow with the radiant, eternal youth of the Other World.

This is the one tale in the present collection in which dazzling beauty is a plot element—but it is the humans who place false value on the illusion of beauty, not Triamor herself. It is clear that Triamor's dazzling beauty is a supernatural attribute. The ability of fairy folk to create an illusion of glamour was well-known to the Celtic people who told and listened to these tales. Actually Triamor's strange beauty is a side issue; the mainspring of the story is Triamor's power to confer fame and wealth. She grants young Lanval his heart's desire and adds the usual taboo to their pact—in this case, Lanval is forbidden to mention Triamor to humans.

The tale is a little more complex than most folk-tales using this basic plot. As usual, the human's impulsive thoughtlessness causes the breakup of the pact and the withdrawal of good fortune. In this tale, Triamor relents at the end and rescues Lanval—if dwelling in the shadowy Other World of fairy folk can be called a rescue. Implicit in the tale is a moral concerning Lanval's fate. Extravagance and thoughtless speech brought about his first misfortunes. Although Triamor rescued him from that state with her magic bounty, this good fortune was again lost through thoughtless speech—a character flaw that may seem minor to us. Nonetheless, Lanval did achieve his dream of wealth and fame for a time, and his departure for the Other World of fairy folk may not be a sad fate after all.

"Finn Magic" is told from the hero's point of view. Although there is no doubt that Zilla is a heroine of strength and courage, hers is a much smaller, though crucial, role. However, the theme of ethnic prejudice is unusual. I felt that the story belonged in this collection, despite the fact that Zilla is seen only through Eilert's eyes. Whatever her role may be in rescuing Eilert from the Draug and Merfolk (the tale is deliberately discreet on this point), it is clear the Nordlanders believed she possessed magic spells or influence over the people beneath the sea. While Eilert may be uncertain about Zilla's magic, he does recognize her physical courage in saving him.

Although I have taken the greater part of this introduction to speak of the remarkably spirited heroines I have culled from the large body of traditional folktales, I cannot end without a few words about the heroes who appear in some of the tales with them. By and large, they are not the stereotyped heroes of most fairy and folktales. They are not flat cardboard characters, but are individually appealing in their own right. Eilert struggles with family loyalty before breaking through prejudice; brave Alexey redeems his mistake of impulsive curiosity; and Lanval is extravagant and thoughtless.

But enough has been said about the quite special heroines—and heroes—in these tales. The proof is in the reading.

THE HUNTER MAIDEN

FEMINIST FOLKTALES FROM AROUND THE WORLD | Vol. IV

MULHA

Long ago in southern Africa, demon spirits and monstrous ogres were much more to be feared than the wild animals of the forests. The ogres were both sly and cruel—they could quickly change their shapes, and were said to devour children.

Mulha, like many other children, had heard tales of the ogre Inzimu and his sister, Imbula. However, it was not until she was fourteen and almost fully grown that she came face-to-face with these monsters. This is the way it happened:

One day Mulha's father was away hunting. Her mother was at work tending the crops in their field, some distance away. Mulha's task was to stay at the family's thatched hut and care for her two younger sisters. Unfortunately, Mulha became quite bored watching the children.

 Her eyes fell on the large storage pot sitting near the door of the hut. The three children had always been forbidden to open this pot, but this day Mulha decided she was going to peek inside. Perhaps, she thought hungrily, her mother kept honey cakes or special treats there.

So Mulha lifted up the heavy lid. Before she could even see the contents, a small, sharp-fanged animal that had hidden there leaped out and grew at once into a huge ogre. When Mulha saw his long tail, she knew he was the ogre Inzimu.

The three girls ran into the hut, the Inzimu after them.

"I won't harm you," said he, making his voice as sweet as honey. "I only want you to cook me some dinner. I'm very hungry."

He persuaded the two older girls to go out for buckets of water; then, as soon as they left the hut, he popped the youngest girl into a large cooking pot and put on a heavy lid.

While the two girls were filling the buckets, a large honeybee buzzed about their heads. The buzzing became words: "The Inzimu has hidden your little sister in the cooking pot!"

4

"How can we save her?" cried the younger sister.

Mulha thought a few moments. Then she said, "After we return, I will run out of the hut. As soon as the Inzimu chases me, you must rescue our sister. Both of you run into the brush behind the hut and hide."

The girls returned with the water and stood quietly near the door. Suddenly Mulha called out in a taunting voice, "You will never catch me, Inzimu!" And she ran out of the hut.

In a rage, the Inzimu started after her. But he tripped over the pail of water the younger sister thrust out, and Mulha had a good start. Fleet as a deer, she dodged the bushes and trees until she reached the river. There she plunged in and swam easily to the other side—for she knew the Inzimu was powerless to follow her over water.

The Inzimu returned to find the small hut empty, and after shouting angry threats of revenge, he departed. But the younger sisters did not creep out of their hiding place until they heard their parents' return.

After Mulha's parents heard the story of the Inzimu who had hidden in the storage pot, they became very alarmed.

"We must leave this hut," declared the father. "Our children are not safe here. The Inzimu will surely return another day. We will go down the valley to my brother's house."

Quickly the family packed up their possessions and left.

"The Inzimu will try to take revenge on Mulha. It was she who tricked him," said the mother. "We must send her away."

To be sure Mulha would be safe, her parents decided to send her to stay with an older married sister living in a distant kraal. Since this was less than a day's walk, Mulha assured her parents she could follow the track to the kraal alone.

Dressed in her best garment, a gaily striped black cloth knotted about her waist, and wearing her brightest ornaments, Mulha set out with a light step. She promised to be very careful and to remember her mother's warning to eat nothing along the way.

It was midsummer, however, and the afternoon was hot. Soon Mulha became very thirsty. When she saw a manumbela tree covered with ripe berries, she could not resist them. Hitching up her skirt, she climbed the tree, and she ate the juicy berries.

As soon as she returned to the ground, the tree

trunk opened. Out came a huge woman, an Imbula, with an ugly animal snout and a hairy red pelt covering her body.

"You are not safe traveling alone," said the Imbula, making her voice as sweet as honey. "You will be robbed of all your pretty things. I will go with you to protect you, but first we must exchange clothes so that you will be safe."

Mulha protested in vain, but the Imbula promised to return everything to Mulha when they approached the kraal. Then she pulled off Mulha's skirt, and in no time at all, she had forced the exchange of clothing.

To her horror, Mulha found that the red, hairy pelt of the Imbula clung to her tightly, as if it were her own skin. The Imbula, wearing Mulha's skirt and ornaments, now looked exactly like Mulha, while Mulha had become an ugly monster!

Not knowing what else to do, Mulha followed the Imbula along the trail. When they approached the kraal, Mulha cried, "Now give me back my clothes!"

Not only did the Imbula refuse, but she walked in through the gate of the kraal with great assurance and asked for her married sister. The sister welcomed the false Mulha warmly.

"What shall we do with this strange creature

with you?" asked the married sister, wrinkling her nose in distaste.

"Put her away in an old hut; she can eat with the dogs," said the Imbula. "It's all she's fit for."

So Mulha, whom her parents had thought the prettiest maiden in Swaziland, was sent to a wretched hut to live with a poor old woman. The Imbula, seemingly a pretty maiden, was made much of by the people in the village. The false Mulha had just one problem: all Imbulas have tails, as Inzimus do, and this she could not get rid of. She had managed to wind hers around and around her waist, where it was hidden by her clothing. Each day she feared it would be discovered, but for a time all went well for the Imbula.

Meanwhile, the real Mulha lived as an outcast in the hut of the old woman. But she did not waste time crying over the cruel revenge taken by the Inzimu and the Imbula. She quickly discovered that the ugly, hairy pelt she wore gave her some magic power; she could obtain choice food simply by commanding it. So, with the old woman sworn to secrecy, the two ate well and lived quietly together in comfort.

Almost every day, Mulha went down early to a deserted part of the river to bathe. As soon as she entered the water, the hairy skin floated away, and she became her own self. She swam happily about for a while, but as she left the water, the skin attached itself to her again, and she became the strange creature as before.

One day the married sister went down to the river to wash some clothes. Catching sight of the strange, hairy woman at the water's edge, she hid herself and watched. What she saw astonished her. She hurried home at once to consult the chief's aging sister, who was well known for her wisdom.

The next time the creature went to bathe, the two women hid near the riverbank. They saw the ugly pelt float away while Mulha swam, and reattach itself when she left the water.

The two women confronted Mulha, demanding an explanation. She told them she was the real Mulha, and explained how she had been tricked by the Imbula.

"If you really are Mulha and the other is not, surely you can prove it!" said the married sister. But it was clear she was not certain in her mind that this was her sister, and Mulha was hurt.

"Why bother with me?" said Mulha. "You took

the Imbula in as your sister; now you can keep her! I have everything I want. Only more trouble will come to me if I accuse the Imbula."

"The girl is right," said the chief's sister. "The Imbula still has power to do her harm. She may take further revenge because Mulha outwitted her brother, the Inzimu. Come away now," said she to the married sister. "We will consult with my brother, the chief, and devise a plan. For the true Imbula must be discovered and killed if Mulha is to be saved."

A few days later a big hole was dug in the middle of the kraal. In it were placed food and a large calabash filled with fresh milk. Each woman in the kraal was commanded to walk all around the hole by herself.

At last came the turn of the Imbula. She begged to be excused. "I am too shy a maiden to walk about before all the people," said she in a tiny, sweet voice. This did not help her at all.

The chief and his sister forced her to begin the walk around the hole. At the sight of the fresh white milk, her Imbula nature could not be controlled. Of its own accord, her tail uncoiled and slithered down into the hole to suck up the milk—for no Inzimu or Imbula can control its tail when milk is on the ground! The chief's sister had known this when she devised the trap.

With a shriek of rage at her unmasking, the Imbula seized a nearby child and leaped toward the gate. But the hunters were waiting with spears ready, and she was slain. The moment the Imbula was killed, Mulha regained her own true form.

After that, Mulha lived peacefully with her sister's family. Eventually she married the chief's youngest son. The one hundred cows paid to Mulha's father as the bride price made it possible for her family to live in great comfort.

And that was how Mulha outwitted the ogre Inzimu and, with the help of the chief's sister, escaped the Imbula's revenge.

"Mulha" is drawn from Fairy Tales from South Africa *(1910), written by* **E. J. BOURHILL** *and* **J. B. DRAKE**. *Versions of this tale have been compared to the story of "Little Red Riding Hood."*

The
HUNTER
MAIDEN

Long ago, among the Zuni people in the Southwest, there lived a young maiden. She lived alone with her aged parents in their pueblo. Her two brothers had been killed in warfare, and it was her responsibility to supply the family with food and firewood.

The little family lived very simply. During the summer, when the girl grew beans, pumpkins, squash, melons, and corn in their garden, they had enough to eat. But when cold weather came, there were only dried beans and corn to feed the family.

The Zuni people did not graze sheep and cattle in those days; therefore to keep hunger at bay through the winter, they had to hunt game. Her brothers' stone axes and rabbit sticks for hunting hung on the walls unused—for it was the custom that only men could hunt, and her father had grown too old and feeble for hunting.

One year the cold weather set in early and the first snow had fallen. Now was the time the girl must gather brush and firewood to store on the roof of their house.

"We have little to eat," she said to herself, "but at least we will be warm."

As she worked, she watched the young men of the tribe go forth with their rabbit sticks and stone axes. Later in the day, she saw them return to the village with strings of rabbits.

"If I were a boy," she thought, "I could hunt rabbits, and my parents would have meat to nourish themselves." She pondered this, saying to herself, "There is no reason why I can't hunt rabbits. When I was a child, my brothers often took me with them on the hunt."

So that evening, as the girl sat by the fire with her parents, she told them she intended to hunt for rabbits the next day.

"It will not be hard to track rabbits in the new snow," she said. "The young men who went out this morning all returned with strings of rabbits, but we have nothing to barter for meat. The rabbit sticks and axes of my brothers are on the wall. Why should I not use them? Must we go hungry again this winter?"

Her mother shook her head. "No, no! You will be too cold. You will lose your way in the mountains."

"It would be too dangerous," said her father. "It is better to live with hunger. Hunting is not women's work."

But at last, seeing that the girl was determined to go, the old father said, "Very well! If we cannot persuade you against it, I will see what I can do to help you."

He hobbled into the other room and found some old furred deerskins. These he moistened, softened, and cut into long stockings that he sewed up with sinew and the fiber of the yucca leaf. Then he selected for her a number of rabbit sticks and a fine stone ax.

Her mother prepared lunch for the next day, little baked cornmeal cakes flavored with peppers and wild onions. These she strung on a yucca fiber, like beads on a string, and placed with the weapons for the hunt.

The girl rose very early the next morning, for she planned to leave before the young men of the village set out to hunt. She put on a warm, short-skirted dress, pulled on the deerskin stockings, and threw a large mantle over her back. The string of corn cakes was slung over one shoulder, the rabbit sticks thrust into her belt. Carrying the stone ax, she set out for the river valley beyond their pueblo.

Though the snow lay smooth and unbroken, it was not deep enough to hinder her. Moving along steadily, she came at last to the river valley, where she climbed the cliffs and canyons on the steep, sloping sides. In and around the rocks and bushes, she saw the tracks of many rabbits.

She followed the tracks eagerly, running from one place to another. At first she had little skill. But remembering all that her brothers had showed her, she at last became skillful enough to add many rabbits to her string.

Snow had begun to fall, but the girl did not heed this, nor did she notice that it was growing dark.

"How happy my parents will be to have food! They will grow stronger now," she said to herself. "Some of the meat we can dry to last many days."

The string of rabbits had grown very heavy on her back when she suddenly realized it was almost dark. She looked about her. The snow had wiped out her trail. She had lost her way.

The girl turned and walked in what she thought was the direction of her village, but in the darkness and the strangeness of the falling white snow, she became confused. She struggled on until she realized that she was completely lost.

"It is foolish to go on," she thought. "I'll take shelter among the rocks for the night and find my way home in daylight."

As she moved along the rocky cliffside, she saw a very small opening that led into a cave. Crawling in cautiously, she found the cave empty. On the floor of the cave were the remains of a fire, a bed of still-glowing ashes. Had another hunter rested here and then left? Delighted with her good luck, she dropped her string of rabbits and hurried to gather twigs and piñon wood from outside. She brought in several armloads to build up the fire for the night ahead.

Sitting down before the crackling fire, she cleaned one of the rabbits and roasted the meat on a spit. With the remaining corn cakes, this made a fine meal. Afterward she lay back on the stone floor of the cave, ready for sleep.

Then, from the dark stillness out on the mountain, came a long, drawn-out call. Thinking it was someone lost in the snow, the girl went to the mouth of the cave and called, "Here!" in answer.

The crackling and snapping of twigs told her someone was coming nearer. Then she heard the sound of a loud rattle and saw the outline of a huge figure.

"Ho!" called a harsh voice. "So you are in there, are you!"

She stood still for a moment, frozen in dismay and terror. Huge red eyes glared at her, and she knew it was one of the Cannibal Demons, who had haunted the world since ancient times. She ran to the back of the cave, crouching down out of sight.

The monstrous Demon was at the mouth of the cave, trying to get in, but the opening was too small for his huge body.

"Let me in!" he roared. "I'm hungry and cold."

The girl did not answer.

Then the Demon called out slyly, "Come out here and bring me something to eat."

"I have nothing for you. I've eaten all my food," the girl answered.

"Bring out the rabbits you caught," he demanded. "I can smell them. I know you have rabbits."

The girl threw out a rabbit. The monster seized it in his long, clawlike hand and swallowed the rabbit in one gulp.

"More!" he demanded.

The girl threw out another rabbit from her string. Again he tossed it into his huge mouth. With a snap of his long, sharp teeth, it went down in one swallow.

"Give me all the rabbits!" he shouted.

Now the girl was angry. "I have no more. Go away!"

The monster swelled with a terrible rage. "I'm coming in there to eat you and your rabbits!"

Again he tried to crawl into the cave, but the opening was too small for even his head to get through. Then he stood up. Lifting his great flint ax, he began to shatter the stones at the entrance. *Clatter*, *pound*, *crash* went the ax on the rocks. Gradually the entrance to the cave became a little larger.

The loud crash of the flint ax on rock traveled clearly through the night air. Far away, on Thunder Mountain, two War Gods heard it. They knew at once that it was the Cannibal Demon's ax, and they knew he was again causing trouble.

Picking up their weapons, they flew through the darkness to the cliffside where the Demon hammered away at the cave entrance. They understood the situation at a glance. Each one swung his war club and hit the Demon on the head. The monster fell to the ground, dead.

"You are safe now, maiden," they called. "We will sleep out here at the entrance to your cave and protect you until morning."

The next day as the sun rose, sparkling the white snow, the girl came out of the cave with her string of rabbits. The two War Gods praised her strength and courage. Then they walked with her down the snow-covered valley to guide her to her village. As they traveled through the fresh new whiteness of the world, the two War Gods taught the maiden much hunting wisdom.

When they could see the pueblo in the far distance, the girl turned to her two companions, bowing low and breathing on their hands to thank them. When she straightened up, they had disappeared.

The girl walked into the village, proudly carrying her string of rabbits. All the people stared at her in wonder. Never had they seen a maiden hunter, and the number of rabbits she had caught astonished them. She did not stop, but hurried on to her own home.

When she entered, her parents cried out in joy to see her unharmed. They feared she had been eaten by a mountain lion.

"Now we have food to eat," she cried. "I'll cook a fine rabbit stew to make you strong. And there will be furs for the bitter cold of winter."

"You have done well, daughter . . . and hunter maiden," her father added, smiling. "From now on you will hunt for our family, and your brothers' axes will be yours."

"The Hunter Maiden" has been adapted from a story in Zuni Folk Tales *(1901), edited by* **FRANK H. CUSHING**. *The cannibal demon in the story appears often in Zuni folklore as Átahsaia: a giant, a trickster, and a liar.*

ELSA
and the Evil Wizard

Long, long ago, a very evil wizard lived in a splendid castle high in the mountains. Outside the castle were large, beautiful gardens filled with bright flowers and delicious fruits.

Scattered throughout the gardens were statues of young maidens so perfect that one would think them alive. And it was a sad fact that once, these statues had been living maidens. For whenever the wizard saw a young maiden who took his fancy, he would cleverly seize her and fly away with her to his castle. There the wizard turned the girl into a stone statue to adorn his gardens.

Whenever he tired of gazing at his collection of statues, he made ready to fly off in search of a new victim. He put on the fine clothes of a nobleman and rubbed his lips with honey to make his voice sweet and beguiling. He sprinkled his cruel face with May morning dew to make it look gentle and kind. Then he wrapped himself in his magic flying cloak. The cloak changed at once into large dark wings, and he flew out over the cliffs and dark pine forests. He circled and dipped, flying lower and lower over the valleys.

If he saw someone he fancied, he would spread his dark cloak on the ground. If a maiden but stepped onto it—even the edge—he would seize her and carry her off. But the wizard's power was not absolute. Unless the victim willingly stepped onto the cloak, he had no power to harm her.

One morning the evil wizard circled and coasted above the valleys longer than usual, for he had a fancy to seek a maiden with long golden hair. At last he saw Elsa walking along a path outside the village with a berry basket on her arm. Her long yellow hair glistened in the sunlight as she bent now and then to pick raspberries.

The gleaming gold drew him downward. He was enchanted. What a fine new statue he would have for his garden! He floated to the ground and took cover behind a clump of hawthorn.

When Elsa drew near, he stepped out and spread his cloak on the path.

"Beautiful maiden," he said, bowing low, "allow me to be of service. Your feet are too dainty and tender to walk on rough, muddy ground. Step onto my cloak."

Elsa laughed. "I'm not a beautiful maiden, and my feet are quite sturdy, thank you! You should take better care of your cloak. How foolish to drop it onto the path! It will be covered with mud."

She picked up the cloak, shook off the dirt, and handed it to the wizard. "You'll ruin your fine cloak, throwing it on the ground for girls to walk on!" With a cheerful smile and a nod, she walked briskly on.

The wizard frowned. He followed behind her at a short distance, wondering how he could trap her.

Some distance ahead he saw a herd of goats grazing, and among them was a powerful billy goat with sharp horns.

"If I make the goat attack her," he thought, "she will run to me for protection. Surely then she will step on the edge of my cloak."

He blew on his magic whistle to attract a swarm of bees. They stung the billy goat about the face. Enraged, the goat tried in vain to butt the bees. Then he caught sight of Elsa. Lowering his horns, he rushed to attack her.

The wizard ran forward with his outspread cloak trailing on the ground. "I will protect you!" he cried.

But Elsa ignored him. She darted behind a bush, the goat after her. Around and around the bush they ran.

The wizard stood by, vexed, waving the cloak with little effect, until Elsa tripped. He quickly threw the cloak down, expecting that she would fall on it. But Elsa rolled to one side, and it was the goat who became tangled in the cloak.

With a blow of his fist, the wizard knocked the goat senseless. Then he angrily pulled his cloak from the horns. The cloak came free, but it had a large rip in it.

When Elsa saw the torn cloak, she felt sorry for him. "Your fine cloak is torn, and all because you tried to protect me," she said kindly. "I'll see what I can do to mend it."

She picked a thin, sharp thorn from a hawthorn bush and, with another sharp thorn, pierced a small hole in the top to make a needle. Then she took a strand of her long yellow hair to use as a thread.

"Hand me your cloak, sir. I will sew the tear as neatly as I can." She sat down, holding the cloak on her knee, and sewed up the tear with the strand of golden hair.

The wizard was not the least bit grateful. When

Elsa handed him the cloak, he shook it out to examine it and complained that the tear needed more stitches. "Look here, how loosely you've sewn it!"

As Elsa moved closer to look, the wizard trailed the corner of the cloak on the ground. Elsa's foot stepped onto the hem!

In an instant, both Elsa and the wizard were wrapped in the cloak. The wizard's face changed to become a face of evil—his eyes were glowing red balls, his cruel mouth showed long yellow teeth, and his arm gripped Elsa's waist. The large dark wings of the cloak spread outward, and Elsa found they were moving upward into the air.

But the strand of yellow hair she had used to sew the cloak caught on a branch of a tree. There it held them fast and did not break.

Try as he would, the wizard could not free them. The more he pulled and tugged, the more the cloak became tangled in the branches. At last, with an angry curse, he used his two hands to pull at the cloak. Freed from his grip, Elsa slid to a lower branch and from there leaped to the ground.

She raced back over the path toward the village and home. Never in her life had she run so fast! She didn't stop until she reached her room and fell upon her bed in complete exhaustion. When she could speak, she told her widowed mother all that had happened.

The wizard flew back to his castle in a terrible rage. He slammed doors, hurled his silver jug across the room to break a mirror, and stormed about the castle so viciously that all his servants hid from him.

That night he lay down on his bed, but he found he could not sleep. The room was strangely bright, and the light hurt his eyes.

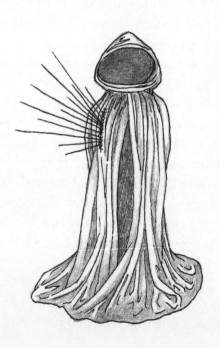

"The moon is shining through the window," he thought. But when he got up to close the shutters on the window, he saw there was no moon in the sky. The bright light was within the room.

Then he saw that the light came from his cloak, which was lying over a chair. The stitches of the mended tear, sewn with Elsa's golden hair, glowed brilliantly against the dark cloak, filling the room with a very bright light.

"Ho!" said he. "So that's the way of it! The stitches will be easy to hide." He rolled the cloak up tightly, with the mended seam inside, and went back to bed.

But again the bright radiance filled the room, shining through the folds of cloth.

"That blasted girl and her golden hair!" he shouted in rage.

He ran down to the castle cellars and hid his cloak under a barrel. It did not help a bit. As soon as he wearily climbed the stairs and fell into bed again, the bright light glowed through all the castle rooms, right up to his bedroom. He was unable to sleep all night.

The next evening his room again glowed with light. He brought the cloak up from the cellars and, with a knife, tried to cut the golden stitches. But he could not cut them.

"Stupid, silly girl!" he kept muttering to himself. "Sewing up *my* cloak with her nasty hair!" In a frenzy, he slashed the mended seam right out of his cloak, leaving a large hole. Then he threw the piece out of the window and went to bed.

But again the brilliant light filled the room. He got out of bed and ran to look at his cloak. The mended tear was back in place, the golden thread still shining brightly.

He knew at last that he had no power to get rid of Elsa's seam.

He did not sleep that night or the next night or the next. After a week he could stand it no longer. He seized his cloak and flew down to the village where Elsa lived. He peered into one window after another until he found her room. He rapped sharply on her window.

Elsa sat up in bed in surprise. "Who's that?"

"It's me. Open your window and talk to me. I won't hurt you."

Elsa recognized the evil voice. She shivered but did not answer.

"Come here, you wicked girl," he cried. "Take your thread out of my cloak. It shines with a horrid bright light and won't let me sleep."

"I will not come to the window," Elsa said. "Go away!"

"I can't sleep, I tell you. For seven nights I've had no sleep! Come, take out your silly hair from my cloak or I'll make you suffer!"

But Elsa's mother had told her the village lore about the evil wizard on the mountain. She knew his only power over her lay in his magic cloak.

When the wizard saw he could not frighten Elsa, he tried another way. "If you take out your thread of hair, I'll give you a sack of gold," he coaxed.

"I don't want your sack of gold," said Elsa.

"I'll give you a large farm filled with sheep as well," he urged.

"I don't want your farm," said Elsa. She didn't trust the wizard an inch. In desperation the wizard offered one fine thing after another. Nothing would make Elsa come to the window.

At last he gave up and returned to his castle in a very bad temper. There he sulked in his garden all the next day, scowling at his stone statues. The statues stared back sadly.

"That silly, stubborn girl has no fear of me," he thought. "What can I do to demonstrate my power?" He conceived the idea of restoring one of his stone statues to life.

As he watched the released maiden run down the mountain path to her home, he thought smugly,

"That will show the foolish Elsa that I am not to be trifled with!"

That night the brilliant light dimmed, and he was able to sleep. But the next night the light from the golden stitches returned as bright as ever.

He flew down to Elsa's window in a rage and rapped sharply to waken her.

"Who's that?" called Elsa sleepily.

"You know very well who it is," he cried. "I've had enough of this nonsense! Don't you know I have powers of enchantment far stronger than your stupid hair? You've had your revenge. Now be a sensible girl and remove the seam."

"I think the seam does very well where it is," said Elsa. And no matter how he blustered or threatened, she would say nothing more.

The wizard flew back to his castle on the mountain. There the bright, piercing light from Elsa's seam would not let him sleep until he restored another of the enchanted stone statues to life.

And so, one at a time, he was forced to free the maidens. Each day that he angrily released a maiden from his garden, the strange light faded, and he slept soundly.

When the last statue was gone, Elsa's golden stitches retained a faint, steady glow—enough to warn the wizard that they would flare up brilliantly if he ever used his evil powers again.

This telling of "Elsa and the Evil Wizard" was inspired by a tale in Old Swedish Fairy Tales *(1925) by* **ANNA WAHLENBERG,** *translated by* **ANTOINETTE DECOURSEY PATTERSON.** *The golden thread, or hair, appears in a number of fairy tales across many countries as a symbol that guides the faithful out of danger.*

MARIA MOREVNA

Long, long ago, when the land of Russia was made up of many small kingdoms, there lived a warrior princess named Maria Morevna.

She had inherited her kingdom from her father, and her father, very wisely, had trained her not only to govern well but also to defend the kingdom against enemy armies. Many princes sought to marry her, thinking to gain control of the land. Maria Morevna refused them all.

One day the young Prince Alexey rode in from the south and said he wished to serve in the army of Maria Morevna. The long and the short of it was, they fell in love, and the marriage took place three months later at the palace, amid great rejoicing. The young couple lived happily together for one year.

Then one day an exhausted messenger rode into the palace courtyard to bring tidings of an enemy attack on the western borders. While the army assembled for war, Maria sat down with Alexey.

"You will rule here in my absence," she told him. "But, dear Alexey, you must never open the door at the top of the east tower."

After a fond farewell, Maria, splendid in her white-and-gold uniform, rode off at the head of her army.

Now, Alexey was consumed with curiosity about the door that must not be opened. He resisted for one day. He resisted for two days. But on the third day he weakened and said to himself, "I'll just take a quick look. Surely that can do no harm."

So he climbed the stairs to the tower. Trying each of the keys entrusted to him until he found the one that unlocked the door, he pushed it open and stepped into the room.

He stood rooted to the floor in astonishment—

for inside was a tall old man with white hair and a long white beard, who stood chained to the wall.

"I am so weak," cried the old man. "Kind youth, will you bring me a jar of water?"

Alexey felt pity for him. He ran down the steps and filled a large jar with water. When he brought it in, the prisoner drank it down in one gulp.

"I feel stronger," said the old man. "Bring me more water, I beg of you."

And so Alexey brought him another full jar of water. This too he gulped down in an instant.

"One more, kind youth," the old man beseeched. Alexey hesitated.

"Bring me one more jar of water, and I promise you I will give you your life when otherwise you must die."

Alexey brought him the third jar of water.

After the prisoner had drained that in a gulp, he swelled in size. As his body grew huge and powerful, his face became cruel and savage. With a quick wrench he broke the heavy iron chains as if they were paper.

"Who are you?" cried Alexey.

"I am Koschei the Wizard," answered the old man exultantly. "Many years ago, the father of Maria Morevna captured me, thinking to rid the country of evil. He destroyed my power and chained me here. Now you have set me free!"

With a swirl of his long cape, he flew out of the window and away. High in the air he flew, like a great bird of prey, till he saw Maria Morevna far below, riding proudly with her army. He swooped down, seized the princess, and flew off with her. He flew over nine times seven kingdoms until he reached his own palace near the sea.

Alexey was crushed with grief. The fate of Maria lay heavily on his heart, for he knew his impulsive carelessness was to blame. While the people of the kingdom mourned their princess, Alexey rode off in search of her.

He traveled many roads for many weeks across many kingdoms before he at last arrived at Koschei's palace. Leaving his horse tethered in the forest, he crept as close as he could. He lay hidden until he saw Koschei ride away on a powerful black horse. Then he climbed a tree and, from an outspread branch, dropped down into the palace garden. There he found Maria Morevna.

They embraced joyfully. But after a moment Maria drew back. "Oh Alexey, why did you disobey my command?" she cried. "Why did you open the room and free the wizard?"

"I was foolish and thoughtless," said Alexey sadly.

"I know it has caused you much grief. But if you can forgive the past, we will set off at once. My horse waits in the forest nearby."

"If it were that easy to escape the wizard, I wouldn't be here now," replied Maria. "He possesses a miraculous horse, and he will catch up with us in a trice!"

"I saw him leave for a day's hunting," urged Alexey. "We can be far away before he discovers you are gone."

But Maria cried, "He will kill you if he catches us—and that I could not bear!"

At last Alexey persuaded Maria to try to escape, for he said he would rather be slain than live without her. So, making their way out of the garden, they mounted Alexey's horse and rode off as fast as the steed could carry them.

In the midst of the hunt, some distance away, Koschei's great horse suddenly stopped in its tracks.

"What ails you, you lazy beast?" cried Koschei, bringing down his whip on the horse's flank.

"Prince Alexey has come and carried off Maria Morevna," said the horse.

Koschei swelled with anger. "After them, you stupid nag!" His spurs dug into the horse cruelly, for he, like many with violent tempers, took out his rage on those who served him.

The horse fairly flew over the ground, scarcely needing the whip and spurs of Koschei. Within a very short time they had overtaken Alexey and Maria.

Seizing Alexey under one arm and Maria under the other, the wizard carried them back to the castle.

"You're a fool. You have no more chance of freeing Maria Morevna than you have of seeing your own ears!" he cried, flinging Alexey to the ground. As the wizard swung his sword high, Alexey cried out, "When I gave you the third jar of water, you promised me my life!"

The sword stopped in midair. "Very well," snarled the wizard. "I will not kill you." And he gave orders for Alexey to be put into a large cask. After the top was tightly sealed, the cask was thrown over the cliff into the sea.

Now, it happened the next day that a hawk, an eagle, and a crow, seeing the cask floating in the sea, became curious and pulled it to shore with their beaks and sharp claws. There they picked at it until they tore it apart.

Great was their astonishment when Alexey crawled out, bruised but unharmed.

Alexey thanked them gratefully, but he added in despair, "I am no more able to free Maria Morevna now that I am outside the cask than when I was inside it!" Then Alexey told his rescuers all that had happened since he unwittingly freed the wizard.

"It is clear," said the crow, "that Koschei's horse is a hundred times swifter than any other."

"Try as often as you will," said the hawk, "he is sure to overtake you."

"You must try to obtain another horse the equal of the wizard's," said the eagle. "Maria Morevna must find out from Koschei where and how he obtained his."

Alexey thanked them for their counsel and set off on foot for the wizard's castle. Once more he waited for Koschei to leave, then climbed into the garden.

Maria was overjoyed to see Alexey still alive. When he told her the advice of the three birds, she nodded.

"Yes," she said, "Koschei likes to boast of his steed's power. Come back here tomorrow, Alexey; let us pray I will have an answer for you."

That evening, Maria spoke of Koschei's horse with great admiration. Then she went on, "Tell me, wise wizard, where was this marvelous steed foaled?"

"On the shore of the blue sea grazes a most wonderful mare. Every three years the mare bears a colt. He who can snatch the colt from the wolves waiting to seize it, and bring the colt safely away, will possess a steed like mine."

"And did you bravely snatch the colt from the wolves?" asked Maria.

"No, it was not I," the wizard admitted. "Near this place lives an old Baba Yaga who follows the mare and snatches each colt from the wolves. Thus she has a herd of many miraculous horses. I spent three days tending them, and for a reward she gave me a little colt. That colt grew up to become the horse I ride."

"How clever you were to find the Baba Yaga!" cried Maria. "It cannot have been easy."

"Only I have that power," boasted Koschei. "One must cross a river of fire to reach her land. I have in my silver chest here a magic handkerchief." The wizard took out the piece of scarlet silk. "I waved this handkerchief three times to my right side and a strong bridge appeared, a bridge so high that the fire could not touch it. What do you think of that, eh?" And he sat back well pleased with himself.

Maria exclaimed at his power and cleverness. Then, in the night, after the wizard was asleep, she went to the silver chest and removed the handkerchief.

The very next day, when Alexey once again stole into the palace garden, she gave the magic handkerchief to him and told him what Koschei had revealed.

Alexey set off at once on his long journey, traveling over wet, mired roads and dry, dusty roads. He found the river of fire and, using the magic scarlet silk, safely crossed on the high bridge.

Now he had to find the Baba Yaga. The land was empty and desolate. He had walked three days without food or drink when, weak with hunger, he came upon a bird with her fledglings. One of these he caught.

The mother bird flew round and round him, squawking desperately. "Do not eat my little one," she cried. "If you will set it free, one day I will do a service for you."

Alexey was moved to pity and set the little bird free.

 Soon afterward he found a wild beehive. He was about to pull out the honeycomb when the queen bee buzzed about his face, saying, "Prince, do not take the honey. It is food for my subjects. Leave it, and in return, one day I will do you a service."

Alexey left the honey and struggled hungrily

on. That evening he came at last to the shore of the blue sea. Here, leaning over the rocks near the shore, he caught a crayfish.

But the crayfish cried out, "Spare my life, Prince. Do not eat me, and one day I will do you a service."

Alexey dropped the crayfish back into the water. He went on so tired and hungry he could scarcely walk.

Not long after this he came to the hut of the Baba Yaga. This hut, as you may know, was set up on high stilts that looked like great chicken legs. He climbed the ladder to the hut and entered.

"Health to thee, Grandmother," he said cautiously.

"Health to thee, Prince," she answered, staring at him with sharp, dark eyes. "Why do you come to visit me?"

"I come to serve you as herder," said he. "I want to graze your horses so I may earn a colt as payment."

"So that's the way it is, eh?" The Baba Yaga sat silent a moment, her brown wrinkled face neither friendly nor unfriendly. "Why not?" she said at last.

"If you tend the horses well, I'll give you a steed fit for a hero. But if you lose even one of them, I'll lop off your head!"

"Hard terms, Grandmother, but I agree."

The Baba Yaga gave him food and drink and a place to sleep in the corner.

The next day the herd was let out of the stables to pasture. At once they raced off in every direction over the wide steppes and disappeared. It happened in the blink of an eye, even before Alexey could mount his horse. All day he searched, but he could not find them.

Just as he gave way to despair, a great flock of birds filled the sky. The birds found the horses, swooped down, and pecking at them sharply, drove them home to the stables by evening. Alexey's kindness in setting the fledgling bird free had been rewarded!

When the Baba Yaga saw this, she was very angry. Secretly she ordered the herd to disappear into the thick forest the next day.

And so it happened on the second day. The horses disappeared into the dense forest. Alexey followed them, but though he searched the forest all day, he could not find them. Wearily he sat down on a log. "I shall never get the colt as payment," he thought in despair. "How will I free Maria Morevna?"

Then suddenly a huge swarm of bees filled the air. They easily sought out the horses, buzzing about their faces and stinging their flanks until all of them fled back to the stable.

That night, while Alexey slept, the Baba Yaga berated the horses soundly, and ordered them to go to the sea the next day and swim until they were completely out of sight.

So it happened on the third day. Alexey, who had followed the horses to the shore, saw them swimming rapidly out to sea. In a trice they had disappeared from sight. Disheartened and weary, he sat down on a rock on the shore. His quest for a steed to rescue Maria now seemed hopeless. He wept, and after that he fell asleep.

It was evening when he was awakened by a crayfish nipping at his finger that was trailing in the water. "The creatures of the sea and shore have driven the horses back. They are safe now in the stable," said the crayfish. "I have served you as I promised. Return now, but hide in the stable—for the Baba Yaga will try to trick you. When the Baba Yaga is asleep, take the shabby little colt standing in the corner and go away at once."

Alexey thanked the crayfish joyfully. He returned to hide in the stable. At midnight, while the Baba Yaga was sleeping soundly, he saddled the shabby colt and rode off. Crossing back over the bridge spanning the river of fire, he found a lush green meadow nearby. Here he grazed the colt at sunrise for twelve mornings. By the twelfth morning, the colt had become a huge and powerful steed. With such a horse as this, he covered the roads back to the wizard's castle in hardly more time than is needed to tell of it.

Maria cried out with joy at the sight of Alexey, but little time was spent in talk. They both mounted Alexey's horse and at once rode off with the speed of the wind.

But the wizard's horse once more faithfully reported Maria's escape. Using whip and spurs, Koschei flew after them.

"You lazy bag of bones," shouted Koschei. "Why don't you overtake them?"

"The horse the prince rides is my younger brother," the wizard's horse replied, "but I will try."

Koschei applied the whip more viciously. As they drew closer to Maria and Alexey, the wizard lifted his great sword to strike.

At that moment the steed Alexey rode cried out to the other, "My brother, why do you serve such a cruel and wicked master? Toss him from your back and kick him sharply with your hooves!"

Koschei's horse heeded the advice of his brother.

He threw his rider to the ground and lashed out with his hooves so fiercely that the wizard was forced to crawl back painfully to the castle on all fours, and he never emerged again.

Maria mounted Koschei's horse, and they returned in triumph to their own kingdom. There they were welcomed with shouts of surprise and thanksgiving.

Very soon after her return, Maria Morevna again mounted Koschei's horse, leading her army forth to root out the invaders in the west. And Koschei's horse served her faithfully ever after.

This telling of "Maria Morevna" is based on a story in Russian Wonder Tales *(1912) by* **POST WHEELER**. *Another version of the tale also appeared in* The Red Fairy Book *(1966) edited by* **ANDREW LANG**. *Prince Alexey appears in a number of other Russian tales as Prince Ivan, frequently engaged in a struggle against his enemy, Koschei.*

It happened one time, in the old days, that the squire of the village needed a new housekeeper. His old housekeeper, Jane, had died, and since her eyes had grown dim in her old age, the squire's hall was now in a sad state.

When the squire hired a crew at cider-pressing time, his eye settled on the strong, sturdy figure of Duffy among the women picking apples.

"Are you needing a job?" said the squire as he paid out at the end of the day.

"I am indeed," said Duffy.

"Can you spin and knit and clean and cook?" asked the squire.

"I make the best meat pies in the village," said Duffy, evading a bit of his question, "but I won't muck out the barns and pigsty."

"I have a man for that," said the squire. "Come

along tomorrow then, for I need someone to take old Jane's place."

Duffy was very pleased with her luck until she saw the inside of the squire's hall. Cobwebs and dirt were everywhere. And though the squire had many bags of his own wool piled in the storeroom, the spinning wheel was covered with dust. There had been neither yarn spun nor clothing knitted for a long time.

"Well," said he carelessly, "there's a bit of work to do here. But first you must spin some yarn and knit me some socks, for my feet are clear out of these."

"And your vest and britches are in no better state," thought Duffy grimly.

"You can get on with it," said the squire. "I'll

be out hunting all the day." And off he went to the stable.

Duffy stood with her hands on her hips, surveying the sad state of the rooms.

"Well," she thought, "I'll clean up a bit, and then I'll make some meat pies."

When the squire returned hungry that night, he happily sniffed the fragrance of meat pies done to a turn. After downing a fair number of them, he stretched out his legs at the hearth.

"My socks now," he said anxiously. "Have you started the spinning of yarn for my socks?"

"Tomorrow," said Duffy.

But the next day when Duffy confronted the huge sacks of wool waiting to be carded and spun, she groaned in dismay. Duffy was a cheerful soul and a good cook, but spinning was not a thing she liked to do—nor had she much skill at it.

"Yarn for the squire's clothes, blankets for the house—there's no end to the spinning and knitting to be done!" she exclaimed as she dusted off the spinning wheel in the kitchen. "The devil himself couldn't do it all!"

"Oh, yes I could!" cried a shrill voice. And out from behind the woodpile at the hearth leaped a small, sharp-featured little man with a long tail.

"Ah, Duffy, my dear, there's no need to work

your fingers to the bone, carding and spinning and knitting, when all can be had just for the wishing of it."

"Oh, it can?" said Duffy suspiciously.

"Spun yarn as fine and strong as metal, knit socks, vests that will never wear out," said he in a coaxing voice. "Blankets, britches, all for the wishing."

Twirling his tail, the little man grinned and waited while Duffy considered the offer.

"There'll be a price for it, no doubt?"

"Nay, Duffy my dear, not a price, but a bargain between us. All the spinning and knitting you wish for three years, and at the end of that time, you come away with me—"

"Humph! Not much of a bargain!" said Duffy.

"Fair's fair. I was going to add," he went on crossly, "that you must come away with me—unless you can guess my name. I always keep my bargains. You have the honest word of a gentleman."

Duffy knew very well that the "gentleman," as he called himself, was a devil. But as she watched the vain little man confidently swinging his tail, she thought, "In three years' time I can get the best of the bargain. It shouldn't be too difficult to find out his name!"

"Agreed," said Duffy.

The little man nodded and grinned—and in the next moment he had disappeared from sight.

Duffy had more sense than to wish for everything at once. When the squire returned from hunting that evening with two fine hares, he sat down before the fire. There were not only steaming meat pies waiting for him but also as fine a pair of long socks as ever was made.

As the months passed, the squire became more and more pleased with his housekeeper. The yarn she produced was of the finest quality; the squire's new vests and britches were as strong as could be. And his long socks! The squire never tired of telling his neighbors of the fine socks Duffy produced for him.

"I've worn these socks for almost a year now," he crowed, "and they're as good as new. Duffy's yarn is as strong as leather."

Duffy kept the devil busily at work and was as pleased as could be with her bargain. She had plenty of time to trot off to the gristmill in the afternoons. There she gossiped cheerfully with the other women of the village as they waited for their grain to be ground. They had a merry time of it, telling old tales and dancing a round or two on the green grass beside the mill.

One evening when the squire came home from his hunting, who should he find in the chimney corner but Huey the widower, who had come a-courting.

The squire frowned and scowled until finally Huey took off.

The next night, Jock, the miller's son, was in the chimney corner.

"What's *he* after?" growled the squire when Jock had left.

"I suppose he's come a-courting and to sample my meat pies," said Duffy.

Almost every evening there was someone sitting in the chimney corner, and it didn't take the squire very long to figure out that the widowers and bachelors of the village all had their eye on Duffy.

"I'll lose my treasure!" he thought in panic. There was only one thing to be done.

"Duffy," said the squire, "would you like to be a squire's wife?"

"I would indeed," said Duffy.

"Then we'd best get married," said he.

Duffy was now the squire's lady, but little else was changed. Aside from wearing finer clothes, she was the same cheerful Duffy, dancing and gossiping with the village women at the mill. She produced the same strong yarn and well-knit clothes. Each evening, when the squire returned from hunting, he found a tasty dinner and an orderly house.

But the three years were running out.

The sharp-faced little man started turning up among the wool sacks, or on top of the kitchen woodpile, jeering, "Only a month more, Duffy my dear, and away you go with me!"

Duffy scowled at him. She had tried every means she knew to find out the gloating devil's name. Not a clue could she find.

"Only two weeks more, Duffy," he said, grinning as he flicked his long tail. "You'll never, never guess my name!" She threw a pot at him, but he vanished immediately and the pot crashed against the wall.

She went off at once to consult her friend Old Bet at the mill.

"I know a thing or two about devils and imps," said Old Bet. "I'll see what we can do."

"Only one more week, Duffy my girl," crowed the sharp-faced little man, popping up beside her in the kitchen. She took a swing at him, but he was gone in an instant and her fist hit the table with a thump.

Rubbing her sore knuckles, she hurried down to Old Bet. "He'll drive me daft with his jeering and his threats," cried Duffy. "I'm that worried! We'll never learn his name!"

But Bet had a plan. "Take a jug of the strongest and best applejack from the squire's cellar and bring it to me at sundown," said Bet.

At sundown the squire was still out hunting. Duffy picked out a large jug of the best jack and carried it down to the green beside the mill.

"Tonight's a full moon," said Bet. "The devils and the witches are gathering to dance at the Devil's Basin out on the moor, and I shall thump the tambourine for them. Come along now before they arrive."

Wrapping herself in a red cloak and picking up the jug and tambourine, Old Bet hurried off with Duffy trotting behind her. When they arrived at the Devil's Basin, a hollow in the moor, it was almost dark.

"Hide yourself well in these furze bushes," ordered Bet, "and whatever happens, do not make a sound."

So Duffy crouched down in the scratchy furze bushes to wait, with barely a peephole through the branches to peer through.

Soon she heard a great rustling and chattering, and she wondered how many witches had flown in to the meeting place. Through her peephole in the bushes she saw a lit fire. It burned with a high blue flame.

Old Bet was seated near the fire, the jug of apple-jack in front of her. She thumped her tambourine and the dancing began.

Round and round the fire went the dancers, and the little devil with the long tail danced with them. Every time he came round, he'd pause to take a deep swig from the jug, until finally he became as loud and merry as a grig.

Roaring with drunken laughter, he jumped up and down, twirling his tail and singing:

>*"Duffy my lady, you'll never guess that*
>*My name is Terrytop, Terrytop, Terrytop!"*

At that moment the baying of hounds hunting hare filled the air. Across the moor in the moonlight rode the squire with his hounds, heading straight for the Devil's Basin.

With a screech and a whoop, the dancers vanished. The tambourine ceased, and the fire died out.

Duffy scrambled out of the furze bushes and ran like the wind for home. She barely had time to stir the stew and settle down, panting beside the fire, when the squire came in.

"What a bad time of it I had this day!" he cried. "Not a hare did the hounds raise till after sundown. And a funny thing happened, Duffy. We chased that hare all over the moor by moonlight until we headed straight for a pack of witches dancing round a fire! What do you think of that, Duffy?"

Duffy shook her head in wonder. "It's bad luck, you know, to break in on witches dancing. What did they do?"

"They up and disappeared in a flash. Nothing left that I could see but an empty jug lying on the moor. Nay, I didn't go close to the place, for I feared the witches' curse." He sighed heavily. "I never did get the hare."

The three years of Duffy's bargain were up. On the appointed day, the sharp-faced little devil appeared in Duffy's kitchen.

"Your time's up, Duffy my dear," said he, smirking and flicking his tail. "I've kept my part of the bargain, now off you go with me."

"Not so fast, sir," said Duffy. "There was more to the bargain than that."

"Ha! You think you can guess my name?" He grinned. "I'll give you three guesses."

"Maybe it is Lucifer?" asked Duffy.

The devil sputtered with laughter and thumped his tail on the floor. "An acquaintance of mine," he said at last.

"Perhaps it is Beelzebub?"

"A cousin of mine, but a low, common sort," he said in disdain. "Come along now. You'll never guess my name—it's not generally known on Earth." And he made as if to lay hands on her.

"Oh, no you don't!" cried Duffy as she dodged out of reach. "Are you honest enough to admit your name is Terrytop?"

The devil stood glaring at her in rage.

"Do you deny your name is Terrytop?" she taunted.

"A gentleman never denies his name," he spat, "but I never expected to be beaten by a minx like you!" And with a puff of smoke he disappeared, never to return.

A moment later, everything in the house that the devil had spun or knitted turned to dust.

When this happened the squire was far away on the moor, hunting as usual. It was a cold day with a piercing wind. Suddenly his long socks dropped off, then his britches, and then every garment that was homespun, till he was clad in nothing at all but his leather shoes and jerkin.

He arrived home blue with cold and shivering like a leaf.

"Ah, Duffy," he said when his teeth stopped chattering and he could speak. "You see what's happened to me! It must be the witches' curse on me for breaking up their dance! Bring me some stockings and britches quickly."

Duffy shook her head sadly. "All the yarn goods

in the house must be cursed as well, for they have all turned to dust!"

When the squire saw that this was true, he groaned at his loss. "But you can spin me some more, Duffy!"

Duffy shook her head again. "It will do no good. You can see that all the spinning and knitting done in this house is cursed. We'd best have the work done elsewhere."

This advice didn't please the squire at all, until Duffy said sensibly, "Would you want all your clothes to drop off out on the moor in the dead of winter—or the blankets on our bed to turn to dust on a cold winter's night?"

The very thought of these disasters was enough to convince the squire. "I'd be a laughingstock in the county, if I didn't freeze to death first!" he muttered.

So the squire's spinning and knitting were done in the village. Duffy was well content with her bargain, and the squire hunted happily ever after.

The Cornish tale "Duffy and the Devil" was adapted from a story in Popular Romances of the West of England *(1865), written by* **ROBERT HUNT**. *The devil, Terrytop, appears in many variations of this fairy tale—most notably "Rumpelstiltskin."*

Lanval
and the
LADY
TRIAMOR

A very long time ago there lived a young nobleman named Lanval, whose only ambition was to be a champion. In all the principal castles of the country, knights competed in jousts and tilting bouts. Lanval longed to win fame as the greatest champion of all.

When Lanval was scarcely eighteen years of age, he came into a comfortable inheritance and set off at once for the castle of the nearest earl. He bought the finest horses and armor, the richest clothes. He was openhanded and generous to everyone. In short, he lived as if there could be no end to his wealth.

Lanval stood well in the earl's favor and was popular with the knights who thronged the earl's castle. He had only one fault: he often spoke impulsively, without thought.

One day the earl announced that he was going

to marry King Ryan's daughter from Ireland. This choice privately dismayed his knights and companions.

"King Ryan's daughter!" exclaimed Lanval impulsively. "I'm sorry to hear that!"

"Are you indeed? What do you have against the lady?" asked the earl.

Lanval now felt uncomfortable and wished he could learn to hold his tongue. Everyone at the castle had gossiped about the lady. Few thought her a wise choice for a bride—but no one had spoken this aloud to the earl.

"It's said she's mean and sharp-tempered," answered Lanval lamely.

"The lady brings a good dowry and is the most beautiful of Ryan's daughters," said the earl coldly. "That is enough for me."

So, with many days of feasting, the marriage took place. But ill-said words travel fast, and the lady took a dislike to Lanval. On the last day of the wedding feast, the new countess gave a lavish gift to each of the earl's knights—except Lanval. This pointed public insult was more than Lanval could bear. He felt his days as companion to the earl were over; there was nothing to do but withdraw from the castle.

Taking a small band of retainers with him, he

rode off aimlessly, staying at one castle after another, jousting in every tournament. And of course he spent money as freely as ever.

Barely a year later he found himself penniless. His retainers, long unpaid, rode away. Unable to pay his bill, Lanval stayed on at the inn where he had lodged. His fine tournament steeds and gear were gone; he had not even money for food. He was in the lowest depths of despair. He could not think what to do.

Borrowing a hack horse for a few hours from the innkeeper's kindhearted daughter, he rode out from the town and into the forest. Here he dismounted and sat down to consider his bleak future.

It was at this point that the Lady Triamor decided to take a hand in Lanval's fortunes. Lanval's youth and ambition had taken her fancy—and women of the fairy world are known to admire openhanded generosity in humans.

Lanval was quite startled to see the Lady Triamor appear suddenly before him. She had all the unearthly radiance and dazzling beauty that fairy women can assume at will. Her garments were of shimmering green, adorned with precious jewels, and her red-gold hair lay like glowing silk over her shoulders. Lanval was enchanted in every sense of the word.

When the Lady Triamor began to speak, it was clear at once that she knew his situation.

"What a pity that a brave and generous knight should be brought so low!" she said. "I would like to help you, dear Lanval."

"I am . . . grateful," stammered Lanval.

 "I can give you what you most desire: a purse full of gold that will never be empty. No matter how many coins you take out, it will always be full. I can give you Blanchard, the finest tournament horse in the world, my banner, and Gifre, my groom. As long as you carry my banner as you ride, you will win every joust and every combat you undertake. No blow can harm you."

Lanval, stunned with joy, was scarcely able to believe his good fortune.

"However, there are certain conditions attached to these gifts. You must forsake all other women and pledge yourself only to me. Although I will be invisible to others, I will come to you whenever and wherever you call me, to be your love. *But remember this*: If you ever speak to any human about me, our pact ends at once."

"Your conditions are easy. I gladly agree to them," said he. "I am already deeply in love with you."

Lanval returned to the inn on the splendid white charger, Blanchard, attended by the groom, Gifre, riding the hack. In Lanval's saddlebag was a heavy bag of gold.

The Lady Triamor's favor brought Lanval all that he had longed for. He won fame as champion in every jousting tournament in the land. In addition, his wealth was unending, and the radiant Triamor came to his chamber whenever he wished.

After several years of traveling about, he returned to visit the castle of his former patron and friend, the earl.

The earl's countess noticed that Lanval, though wealthy, was still unmarried; although he was courteous to all the young ladies of the court, he favored none of them.

Seeking him out when he was alone, the countess said to him spitefully, "None of the fine ladies here seem to please you. I think it very strange that after all these years you love no woman, and no woman loves you!"

Alas, Lanval still had not learned to hold his tongue.

"That's not true," he retorted. "I have my own lady, far more enchanting than anyone here!"

"I doubt that!" sneered the countess, for she was extremely vain about her looks. "Although you've won fame and fortune, no one has seen this lady you speak of. Do you hide her away because she is so ugly and ill-favored?"

"My Lady Triamor is the most beautiful woman in the world!" cried Lanval angrily. "Next to her, all the ladies in this castle are plain and dowdy!"

This insult was of course unforgivable, and the countess rushed at once to the earl.

Lanval returned to his chamber, ashamed of his thoughtless temper. There he found that his bag of gold was empty. When he looked out the window, he saw Gifre, holding Triamor's banner, trotting away from the castle on Blanchard.

The full weight of the disaster struck him like a blow. All was lost, including his Lady Triamor. He was penniless again.

It was not long before fresh disaster overwhelmed Lanval. He was summoned to the earl's presence to answer charges before the assembled court.

The countess charged that Lanval had asked to be her lover and that when she had angrily repulsed him, he had said she and all the ladies of the castle were plain and dowdy. Both insults were intolerable. The countess demanded Lanval's death.

Needless to say, the earl was furious at this abuse of his friendship and hospitality. He listened to Lanval's explanation but did not believe him.

"I swear I did nothing—said nothing of love to the countess!" Lanval pleaded. "I said my Lady Triamor was so enchantingly beautiful she would make the ladies of the castle seem plain. I apologize to the ladies for my discourteous words. But I spoke only the truth about my Lady Triamor!"

Many of those assembled in the great hall for the trial were friends of Lanval. They knew him to be thoughtless and impulsive—but also generous and honest. In addition, they knew the mean temper of the countess.

"If the knight Lanval spoke only the truth about his own lady, surely he should not be punished by death!" they cried.

At last the earl was persuaded that this was fair. Lanval must produce his Lady Triamor, and if all agreed she was as radiant in beauty as Lanval claimed, he would be pardoned.

Sadly, Lanval returned to his chamber. He tried again and again to summon Triamor, but she did not appear. Their pact was broken.

The earl had given Lanval seven weeks to produce his lady. As the time passed, Lanval's friends eyed him anxiously. The countess wore an air of smug triumph. And all Lanval could do was to ride hopelessly through all the forests in the earl's domain, searching for Triamor.

When the seven weeks had passed, the earl and the court assembled in the great hall to pass judgment on Lanval.

"I cannot bring my Lady Triamor before this court," confessed Lanval. "I love her dearly, but I broke my word to her, and she has forsaken me."

A deep sigh of sorrow rippled through the company. Lanval was doomed.

Just then a cry rang out: "Look! Someone comes!"

Through the great open archway of the entrance, they could see a party of riders coming toward the castle. A buzz of speculation rose from the company.

Over the drawbridge the Lady Triamor rode with seven attendants, all clad in jeweled cloth of gold. Each maiden was lovely, but the golden radiance of the Lady Triamor stunned and dazzled all who gazed at her.

"Is this your lady?" asked the earl when he could find his voice.

"This is my Lady Triamor." Lanval went to her and knelt down for forgiveness.

So powerful are the enchantments of fairy women that all the company in the hall stood transfixed. Not one could deny that Triamor was more dazzling than any woman in the world.

"The knight Lanval is freed of the charge against him," said the earl.

Triamor motioned for Lanval to leap up behind her on her horse. When he was seated, the party turned and rode out of the castle. As long as they were in sight, no one could move or speak a word.

Where they went nobody knows, for young Lanval was never seen again in this world.

"Lanval and the Lady Triamor" is a Breton story of Lanval, a knight in King Arthur's court. This version was drawn from fourteenth- and fifteenth-century manuscripts by the poet **MARIE DE FRANCE** *that were edited and printed in scholarly collections during the nineteenth century. Another more recent edition of the tale is* Middle English Verse Romances *(1966), edited by* **DONALD SANDS**.

BENDING WILLOW

Long ago, the young Seneca maiden Bending Willow lived together with her parents, not far from the great falls called Niagara. The tribe was at peace, and the waterfowl and fish from the river were plentiful. But Bending Willow was very unhappy.

Although several young warriors sought her in marriage, the most persistent and most unwelcome suitor was the chief, a cruel old man rightly named No Heart. His hair was as gray as a badger, and he had already buried three wives. However, he had great power in the tribe, and when he declared that he would take Bending Willow for his next wife, her parents dared not refuse him.

Bending Willow had another reason for sadness; she had no living brother or sister to help or advise her. They had died from the mysterious sickness that so often attacked members of the tribe. Since her close friend, Laughing Water, had been taken, Bending Willow felt very much alone.

The tribe blamed an evil spirit loose in the village for the mysterious sickness. Chief No Heart proclaimed that the marriage celebration of a chief would drive away this evil spirit. Then he set the day for the ceremony.

When Bending Willow was told of this, she ran into the forest to be alone and think. She would not marry Chief No Heart. She did not believe the mysterious sickness would disappear if the marriage took place. At last she could think of only one solution: she must leave the village and escape to the lands across the wide river.

Early the next morning before dawn, when all were sleeping, she dragged her father's canoe to the edge of the river, stepped into it, and paddled swiftly out into the current.

The night was still dark, with very few stars gleaming in the blackness above her, and the current at this time of the year was much stronger than she had expected. She paddled with all her strength for some time without success. Instead of making her way across the wide river, she found herself at dawn headed toward the rapids.

The paddle was torn from her hands as the canoe tossed about wildly, like a withered branch, on the white-crested waves. The roar of the great falls filled her ears. Swiftly but surely she was borne toward the rocks at the edge of the great falls.

She raised her eyes to the distant star still gleaming steadily in the morning grayness above. If only the Star Maiden would lift her up to the heavens!

"I would rather be up in the sky forever than down at the bottom of the river!" she thought.

For one moment only, she saw the bright white-and-green foam of water. Then she felt herself lifted on great white wings above the rocks. The water divided, and she passed into a dark cave behind the foaming spray.

In the cave was a small creature with a white face and hair of soft white mist, like the mist that rises from the base of the falls. It was the water spirit Cloud-and-Rain, who had rescued her and taken her into his lodge. The door of his lodge was the green wave of Niagara, and the walls of the cave were of gray rock studded with white stone flowers.

Cloud-and-Rain gave her a warm wrapper and seated her on a heap of ermine skins in a far corner where the dampness was shut out by a magic fire. He brought her fish to eat and delicate jelly made from mosses only the water spirits can find.

When she was rested, Cloud-and-Rain told her he knew her story. "No Heart is not a wise leader for your people," he said. "The campsite of the village is a bad one. It is too close to the swamp. When the sickness came, he did not listen to the elders' advice to move."

"You know of the mysterious sickness!" cried Bending Willow. "It has taken my brothers and sister and my friend Laughing Water. No one knows what evil spirit brings it or how to drive it away!"

"There are herbs to help and knowledge of how to use them. That I can teach you." Cloud-and-Rain was silent for a time. "Yes, there are many things I can teach you that will help your people. The water of your village is bad, poisoned."

"Poisoned?" Bending Willow stared at him in perplexity. "What evil spirit did that? I do not understand."

"Listen carefully if you wish to save the lives of your tribe," said the water spirit Cloud-and-Rain. "A great serpent lies underneath the ground of your village. He poisons the springs from which you draw the water to drink. When people die, the serpent is pleased, and more and more poison seeps into your springs. Even now the spring that No Heart uses is fouled, and he will soon die."

"If you can teach me how the village can get rid

of this evil serpent, I will stay with you gladly," said Bending Willow.

"When you return," said Cloud-and-Rain, "you must persuade your people to move their camp. Let them come to dwell nearer to me, in the high upland."

Bending Willow stayed three months with Cloud-and-Rain. He taught her much medicine skill and showed her the herbs to cure sickness.

One day when he came in from fishing, he said to her, "Chief No Heart is dead. This night I will throw a bridge from the foot of the waters across the falls to the high hills. You must climb it without fear, for I will hold it firmly until you are on the land."

When the moon rose, casting a gleam of silver on the waters, Cloud-and-Rain caused a gentle wind to raise the spray until it formed a great white arch reaching from his cave to the distant hills. He led Bending Willow to the foot of this bridge of mist and helped her start off. Higher and higher she climbed, brave and confident, until she descended the misty arch onto the high upland.

When she returned to the village, the tribe welcomed her joyfully. No one blamed her for leaving the tribe to escape marriage with No Heart. They listened quietly when she told them of the water spirit Cloud-and-Rain and of the medicine wisdom he had taught her. But they would not agree to move their village to the uplands.

"The swamp is a protection against enemy attack," they said, "and there are plentiful fish and waterfowl here."

"The upland farther down the river is safer," she answered. "The water is pure. There are many herbs and plants to cure sickness. Here the water springs are poisoned by an evil serpent spirit who lies hidden under the ground." But they shook their heads in disbelief.

When the tribe would not accept the wisdom she had brought from the water spirit, Bending Willow at first felt discouraged. But the months she had spent with Cloud-and-Rain had given her confidence and courage, as well as wisdom. She spoke to her mother and other women of the village separately. Several of them were persuaded that the water spirit's advice was sound.

Bending Willow led these women to the high uplands to draw their water from the clear springs bubbling out from the rocks. Then the women carried the water carefully back to the village. They did this for several months. Neither the women nor any of their families who used this water fell ill. Of those using the village water, some sickened—

among them were strong warriors as well as two of the new chief's children.

This was enough to convince the new chief. The tribe held a council and voted to move. They took down their lodgepoles and moved the village to the uplands.

There the tribe lived in peace and good health. Bending Willow shared her knowledge of herbs with the women of the tribe. And before many months had passed, she happily married a young warrior of her choice.

The poisonous serpent in this story appears in other Seneca folklore and mythos, often to signify displacement. This retelling of "Bending Willow" draws inspiration from American Indian Fairy Tales *(1895), edited by* **MARGARET COMPTON**.

FINN
Magic

Far to the north, on the bleak coast of the Northern Seas, there once lived a lad named Eilert. His family were fisher folk, and they lived beside a rocky headland jutting out into the sea. Their nearest neighbors, who lived some distance along the shore on the other side of the cliff, were a family of Finns.

Both Eilert's family and the Finns used the same fishing grounds, but there was no friendliness between them. Eilert's family were Nordlanders, and they were sure the Finns used their special magic against them.

Eilert's father muttered angrily, "Heathen charms and spells!" when the Finns hauled in a good catch and his own was small.

The Nordlanders along that coast thought the Finns were strange folk with a knowledge of ancient magic. The Finns had black hair, wore odd clothes, and talked among themselves in a peculiar language. All their habits and customs were strange, and their burial ground in the village was separate and apart from the Nordlanders' graves.

Eilert did not share his father's fear of the Finns' magic. When he was a small child playing on the rocky headland, he had met Zilla, a Finn girl his own age. They had become friends, and he had often gone home with her to the Finns' place on the other side of the headland. Zilla was thin and wiry, but she was strong. She could run like a hare and handle a boat as well as he could.

The Finns were kind to him. He saw no evil in them. Nonetheless he thought it best not to tell his family where he had been whenever he returned from a visit to Zilla's place.

Nor did he tell his family of the strange tales the Finns told of Mermen and Draugs who dragged fishermen under the waves to their homes at the bottom of the sea. The Mermen had heads like seals; the Draugs were evil creatures with heads of seaweed.

Eilert and the Nordlanders knew of course that Mermen lived under the Northern Seas, waiting for victims. But the Finns seemed to have an uncanny knowledge of this kingdom beneath the sea, and claimed that their ancestors had often visited there.

Walking home across the headland after hearing these tales, Eilert shivered and wondered if the Finns did indeed have a strange power over the sea. But the lass Zilla was friendly and merry, and the Finns seemed to be kind, cheerful folk, so he put the thought away from him.

Now it happened that one autumn Eilert's family was having a very lean time of it. Day after day on the fishing grounds his father's lines caught next to nothing, while not far off, a dark-haired Finn pulled up one fine catch after another. Eilert's father swore the Finn was making strange signs in the air and using magic spells against him.

"I'd use our counter-charm," cried his father angrily, "but I don't dare. It's said the Merfolk take a terrible revenge on those who do!"

Eilert became very troubled. Was the Finn using magic to lure all the fish to his lines? He felt guilty about his secret friendship with Zilla and the Finns—could this be the cause of his father's bad luck?

He stopped his visits to the Finns' place, and he no longer walked with Zilla under the pines on the headland. But this did not help at all. Day after day, Eilert's father set out his lines and drew them in almost empty of fish.

Eilert knew the counter-charm was dangerous,

for it put the user in the power of the Merfolk. But he made up his mind that he himself must use it. He must take earth from the grave of a Finn and rub it on his father's fishing line.

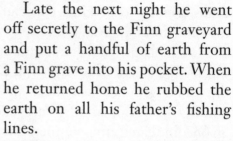

Late the next night he went off secretly to the Finn graveyard and put a handful of earth from a Finn grave into his pocket. When he returned home he rubbed the earth on all his father's fishing lines.

The very next day his father hauled in a fine catch, and this good luck continued day after day. The counter-charm had worked. But each day Eilert's fear of the Draugs and Merfolk increased. To avoid their revenge, he went back to the Finn grave one night to beg forgiveness. But he also took care to carry a piece of iron in his pocket at all times, as protection against sorcery.

One day Eilert went out alone to fish for Greenland shark, for the fish brought a fine price at market. As he rowed, he did not look in the direction of the Finns' place, nor did he notice the lass Zilla watching him from the shore. He rowed on out of sight.

When a shark at last took his line, it was a huge one. Although the boat was small, Eilert would not give up his efforts to pull the shark alongside. At last the shark tore off with Eilert's line taut behind him. Then, unable to lose the fishing line, the shark twisted and plunged suddenly down to the depths of the sea. The boat capsized.

Faint and numb with cold, Eilert clung to the hull of the overturned boat as it tossed in the rough sea. Suddenly he saw, sitting on one end of the boat, a large creature with a seaweed head and a neck like a seal. The two reddish eyes glared at him. The Draug slowly forced its end of the boat down under the water.

"You rubbed your lines with grave earth," hissed the Draug. "Now the people of the sea seek their revenge."

Eilert closed his eyes in despair. He felt himself sinking down under the waves. When he opened his eyes, the frightening Draug was gone, but he saw that he was standing on the bottom of the sea near his overturned boat.

The floor of the sea was made of white sand, and the light around him was pale gray, but strangely he did not feel cold or wet. Then he saw a Mermaid beside him.

"I have rescued you from the Draug," she said. "Come, now I must take you to my father, the king of the Merfolk."

The Mermaid's black seaweed hair floated out

from her head; her face was pale, with dark, gleaming eyes. Her form was clad in a greenish substance, and the silver brooch she wore had the same strange design the Finns used.

Eilert walked with the Mermaid along the sandy bottom. On either side were meadows of sea grass and bushes of thick seaweed. They passed brightly colored shells and broken hulls of boats half buried in the sand.

At last they came to a house made from the hulls of two ships. The Mermaid led Eilert through the door, which she closed behind him. Inside, seated on a rough chair, was a large Merman. His head and neck were like a seal's, but his face resembled that of a dogfish. The fingers on both hands were webbed together, and his feet were covered in old sea boots.

"Well, Eilert," said the Merman, grinning, "you've had a very bad time of it up there today. Sit down, sit down."

Eilert saw nowhere to sit but on a pile of old nets. When he was seated, the old Merman shook his head sadly. "You should not have taken our grave earth to rub on your lines. But you're here now, so you might as well make the best of it."

Eilert could think of nothing to say. He put his hand into his pocket to touch the piece of iron.

The Merman brought out a jug of strong Northern brandy.

"Drink up! Drink up!" he cried, pouring the brandy into cups.

Eilert drank one cup, then another. He decided he had had enough. But the Merman drank merrily on, finishing one jug after another while the dark-haired Mermaid stood silently at the door.

At last the Merman sighed and leaned back with glazed eyes. Without a sound, he slid slowly to the floor and slept.

"Come," said the Mermaid. "He will sleep like that for hours."

He followed her back along the sea floor until they reached his boat where it lay on the sand.

The Mermaid turned to him. "If I am to help you escape and return to the world above, you must lie down in the boat now and sleep."

Eilert hesitated, but the Mermaid's eyes were as kind as Zilla's and he was very tired. He lay down in the boat and closed his eyes. He felt her black seaweed hair spread around him like a dark curtain. As he drifted off to sleep, he heard her chanting a strange song.

When Eilert opened his eyes, he looked about in wonder. He was safe in the Finns' house, and Zilla and her father sat close by. Zilla's long black hair lay over her shoulders; her dark eyes stared at him from her pale face.

"I was under the sea with the Merfolk," he cried. "How—how—" The room was still. Zilla and her father exchanged glances. Then the old man said evasively, "Aye. Our Zilla brought you back. She knows a thing or two about the sea, does Zilla!"

So it was Zilla who had saved him! Eilert wondered what powers she had used. He thought it best not to question; it was enough to know she had rowed out to sea to bring him home.

Now when a lass, Finn or Nordlander, sets about rescuing the lad of her choice—whether by magic or otherwise—there can be only one outcome. The following spring, Zilla and Eilert were married.

It was the first time a Nordlander had married a Finn, and everyone in the village was surprised. But Eilert's parents, on thinking the matter over, had concluded that if the Finns did indeed possess magic spells over fish and other creatures of the sea, it was much better to have them in the family than not.

"Finn Magic" has been adapted from a Norwegian legend told in Weird Tales from Northern Seas *(1893) by* **JONAS LIE**. *Norwegian, Japanese, and Irish folktales all share recurring stories of underwater fairylands inhabited by ethereal beings, merfolk, and the spirits of those who have drowned.*

The OLD WOMAN
and the Rice Cakes

Long ago in Japan, there was a cheerful old woman who lived alone in a small house halfway up a steep hill. She had a few chickens and a pig, but very little else. Quite often she had only one meal a day.

One evening she had just finished making a small bowl of round rice cakes for her dinner, when the bowl slipped and the rice cakes fell to the floor. To her dismay, they rolled right out the doorway. The old woman ran after them.

Once outside, the rice cakes rolled down the steep hill, bouncing over rocks, going faster and faster. The woman scurried down the hill behind them, but she could not catch up with them until they came to rest at the very bottom, near a large slab of rock.

Just as the woman bent over to pick up her rice

cakes, a long, blue, scaly arm with a three-fingered, clawlike hand reached out from behind the rock and snatched them from her.

"That's my dinner!" she cried. She peered behind the rock slab, and seeing a small opening, in she went, right after her rice cakes.

She found herself in a narrow tunnel. Ahead of her was a large, shambling creature hurrying away.

"Sir!" she called loudly, trotting after him. "My dinner! You've taken my dinner!" But the creature went right on, with the woman close behind him, until they reached a large cave.

The old woman stopped short in surprise. In the cave were several more large creatures. They had horns on their heads, wide mouths that stretched from ear to ear, and three red, staring eyes. She realized she was in a den of Oni, ogres who lived under the ground and came forth only at night. The Japanese Oni, like trolls and demons in other parts of the world, are always bent on evil mischief.

She was, however, more angry than frightened, for the Oni had greedily shared her rice cakes among themselves and gulped them down.

"You're no better than thieves!" she cried. "You've eaten my rice cakes and now I have no dinner!"

But they only sat licking their large, clawlike hands, staring at her so hungrily that she wondered if they were going to eat her next.

Then one of them said, "Did you make the rice cakes?"

"Yes, I did," retorted the old woman. "I make very tasty rice cakes, if I do say so myself."

"Come along, then, and make more!" said he, and he clumped away through a maze of tunnels and caves. The old woman followed him, for she was by now quite hungry, and she thought it only fair that the ogres should give her dinner.

But by the time they arrived at the cave full of huge round cooking pots, she realized she was hopelessly lost. She doubted she could ever find the small hole in the rock where she came in.

The Oni dropped a few grains of rice into a large pot of water.

"That will never make enough rice cakes!" she said crossly.

"Of course it will, stupid creature," he scowled. He picked up a flat wooden stirrer. "Put this into the pot and start stirring."

The woman did as she was told. At once the few grains of rice increased until almost the whole pot was filled. So the old woman made the ogres a huge pile of rice cakes—taking care to eat some herself first, before handing them over.

"I'll be going home now," she announced firmly, "if you'll show me the way back to the entrance."

"Oh, no," growled the Oni. "You will stay here and cook for us."

This did not suit the little old woman at all, but as she looked at the large monsters crowded about, licking their claws, she thought she had better not say so.

Nevertheless, while the woman worked to make piles of rice cakes for the hungry Oni, she thought and thought about how to escape. She soon discovered that the source of the water for cooking the rice was a stream nearby, flowing along between the rock caverns. She thought this must be the same stream that flowed out of the bottom of the hill below her home. Farther on, it became a river, and the people of the village fished from its banks.

But there was no boat to be seen.

"The Oni would not have a boat," thought the old woman. "It's well-known the wicked creatures cannot go over water!"

Without a boat, how could she escape? She thought of this as she cooked and stirred—until she saw that one of the large round pots might do very well. They were as big as she was.

The Oni, being night creatures, slept during the day, sprawled in the many caves under the hill. The next day, as soon as they were all asleep, she put the magic stirring paddle in a huge pot and dragged the pot down to the stream.

It floated very nicely, so she hopped in and started to paddle. But the grating sound of the pot being dragged to the stream had wakened a number of Oni nearby. Suddenly they appeared on the side of the stream, shouting in rage.

The old woman paddled faster and faster. Ahead she could see a patch of sunlight where the stream made its way out into the world.

But the stream began to shrink, growing smaller and smaller. Then she saw that the Oni were drinking up the water, swelling up like monstrous balloons as they sucked in the stream. Rocks and stones began to show in the bed of the stream. The huge pot ground to a halt. All around her, stranded fish flopped about helplessly on the stones.

It seemed the ogres could soon walk across the gravel to seize her. Quick as a wink, the old woman picked up the fish and tossed them, one after another, to the ogres on the banks.

"Have some fish stew!" she called.

The Oni caught the fish in their claws—and because they were always hungry, they opened their wide mouths to gulp down the fish. As soon as they did this, the water rushed out of their mouths again, back into the stream—which, of course, was just what the old woman had hoped would happen.

The round pot floated free, and off the old woman paddled, out of the hill and into broad daylight.

When she had floated down the stream to a safe distance, she paddled over to the nearest bank. Hopping ashore, she pushed the big pot back into the water to drift farther downstream. This, she thought, would mislead the Oni if they should come looking for her. But she kept the magic stirrer with her and climbed safely back up the hill to her house.

The old woman never went hungry again, for with the magic stirrer she was able to make as many rice cakes as she could eat—and she had enough left over to share with her neighbors.

But if any rice cakes fell to the floor and rolled away down the hill, she never went after them.

"Let the Oni have them," she'd say cheerfully. And so, with her chickens, her pig, and plenty of rice for her dinner, she lived very happily the rest of her days.

Oni are often depicted in Japanese folktales as cruel and gruesome beasts but can also be considered ambivalent beings, containing both good and evil. The editor's source for this retelling is Tales of Laughter *(1908) by* **KATE D. WIGGINS;** *another version of this tale is also found in* Japanese Fairy Tales *(1918) by* **LAFCADIO HEARN**.

The HUSBAND Who Stayed at Home

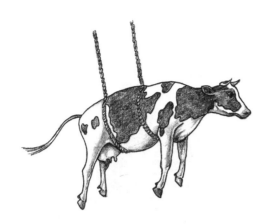

Once upon a time there was a man so cross and bad-tempered that he thought his wife never did anything right in the house.

So one evening during the haymaking time, when he came home scolding and complaining, his wife said, "You think you could do the work of the house better than I?"

"Yes, I do," growled the husband. "Any man could!"

"Well, then, tomorrow let's switch our tasks. I'll go with the mowers and mow the hay. You stay here and do the housework." The husband agreed at once. He thought it a very good idea.

Early the next morning his wife took a scythe over her shoulder and went out to the hayfield with the mowers; the man stayed in the house to do the work at home.

He decided first to churn the butter for their dinner. After he had churned awhile, he became thirsty; he went down to the cellar to tap a pitcher of ale. He had just taken the bung out of the ale barrel and was about to put in the tap when overhead he heard the pig come into the kitchen.

With the tap in his hand, he ran up the cellar steps as fast as he could, lest the pig upset the butter churn. When he came up to the kitchen, he saw that the pig had already knocked over the churn. The cream had run all over the floor, and the pig was happily slurping it.

He became so wild with rage that he quite forgot the ale barrel in the cellar. He ran after the pig, slipped, and fell facedown into the cream.

When he scrambled to his feet, he caught the

pig running through the door and gave it such a kick in the head that the pig dropped dead.

All at once he remembered the ale tap in his hand. But when he ran down to the cellar, every drop of ale had run out of the barrel.

There was still no butter for their dinner, so he went into the dairy to look for more cream. Luckily there was enough cream left to fill the churn once more, and he again began to churn butter.

After he had thumped the churn for a while, he remembered that their milking cow was still shut up in the barn. The poor cow had had nothing to eat or drink all morning, and the sun was now high in the sky.

He had no time to take the cow down to the pasture, for the baby was crawling about in the spilt cream, and he still had to clean up the floor and the baby. He thought it would save time if he put the cow on the top of their house to graze. The flat roof of the house was thatched with sod, and a fine crop of grass was growing there.

Since the house lay close to a steep hill at the back, he thought that if he laid two planks across the thatched roof to the hill, he could easily get the cow up there to graze.

As he started out the door he realized he should not leave the churn in the kitchen with the baby crawling about. "The child is sure to upset it!" he thought.

So he lifted the churn onto his back and went out with it.

"I had best give the cow some water before I put her on the roof to graze," he said to himself. He took up a bucket to draw water from the well, but as he leaned over the well to fill the bucket, all the cream ran out of the churn, over his shoulders, and down into the well.

In a temper, he hurled the empty churn across the yard and went to water the cow. Then he searched for two planks to make a bridge from the hill to the roof of the house. After a great deal of trouble, he persuaded the cow to cross the planks onto the sod roof.

Now it was near dinnertime, and the baby was crying. "I have no butter," he thought. "I'd best boil porridge."

So he hurried back to the kitchen, filled the pot with water, and hung it over the fire. Then he realized the cow was not tied; she could easily fall off the roof and break her legs.

Back he ran to the roof with a rope. Since there was no post to tie her to, he tied one end of the rope around the cow, and the other end he slipped down the hole in the roof that served as a chimney. When he came back to the kitchen he tied the loose end around his knee.

The water was now boiling in the pot, but the oatmeal still had to be ground for the porridge. He ground away and was just throwing the oatmeal into the pot when the cow fell off the roof.

As she fell, the rope on the man's knee jerked, and he was pulled up into the air. The pot of water was knocked over, putting the fire out, and the man dangled upside down above the hearth. Outside, the poor cow swung halfway down the house wall, unable to get up or down.

In the meantime, the wife had mowed seven lengths and seven breadths of the hayfield. She expected her husband to call her home to dinner. When he did not appear, she at last trudged off to their home.

When she got there, she saw the cow dangling in such a queer place that she ran up and cut the rope with her scythe. As soon as the rope was cut, the man fell down the hearth.

His wife rushed into the house to find her husband in the hearth, covered with ashes, the floor slippery with clots of cream and ground oatmeal, and the baby wailing.

When they had cleaned up the house, taken the cow out to pasture, and hung up the pig for butchering, they sat down to eat stale bread without butter or porridge.

The wife said to him, "Tomorrow you'll get the right way of it."

"Tomorrow!" he sputtered. "You'll not be going out with the mowers tomorrow!"

"And why not? You agreed to it," said she. "Do you think the work of the house too hard?"

This the husband would not admit. "No indeed! If you can do it, I can do it!" he growled.

"Well, then!" said his wife.

They argued the rest of the day over who should mow and who should mind the house. There seemed no way to settle it until at last the husband agreed that he would work in the fields three days a week and work in the house three days; his wife would take his place in the fields for three days and take care of the house the other days.

With this compromise they lived quite peaceably, and neither the husband nor the wife complained very much at all.

"The Husband Who Stayed at Home" has been adapted from Popular Tales from the Norse *(1859) by* **PETER CHRISTEN ASBJØRNSEN** *and* **JØRGEN MOE**, *translated by* **G. W. DASENT**. *Family members trading roles, with humorous and chaotic results, is a theme often explored in folktales from around the world.*

SCHEHERAZADE
Retold

A very long time ago, a young woman named Scheherazade lived in the lovely city of Samarkand. It was a city of fragrant gardens, elegant marble fountains, and heavily laden fruit trees. But a dark shadow of fear lay across the city, for a cruel Sultan ruled there.

Scheherazade's father was one of the Sultan's chief advisers. Thus the shadow of fear did not touch her directly, but it lay heavily upon every other family in the city who had a daughter, and Scheherazade shared their grief and terror.

In truth, it seemed as though the Sultan had gone mad. Suspecting that the Sultana had been unfaithful, he had had her put to death. Since then, he had demanded that young maidens of the city be brought to him, one after another, as brides. But each "bride" lasted scarcely more than a day or two before she either bored or enraged the Sultan—and she was thrown into a dark dungeon. Many of the daughters in the city had already disappeared, and those who remained lived in terror.

Scheherazade was deeply troubled and turned over in her mind what could be done to stop the Sultan's reign of terror. She was well-educated in all areas of history and literature, for her father had provided her with the best tutors in the country. But more to the point, she was clever and courageous as well.

One day she said to her father, "I have a favor to ask of you."

"I can refuse you nothing," said he affectionately.

"I am determined to stop this barbarous behavior of the Sultan. As long as this terrible fate hangs over us, no woman in the city is safe."

"That is true," said her father heavily. "But how can you stop him? Neither the pleas of his advisers nor the heavy grief of the people have any effect."

"Today the Sultan has demanded that a new maiden must be sent to his chambers in the palace. I want you to tell him that I am willing to go," she answered calmly.

"Have you lost your senses?" cried her father in horror. "He is a half-mad old man!"

"Someone must free the women of the city from this evil," she replied. "I have a plan as to how this may be done."

He shook his head in anguish. "If you do not care about your fate, think of the grief it would cause me. You are the pride of my heart. You have had the finest masters to teach you. With all your cleverness and learning, how can you wish to sacrifice yourself?"

"The Sultan's vicious behavior must be stopped," she repeated. "No woman in the city, or the country, will be safe until it ends. How can I sit here with my books and do nothing?"

Her father continued to plead with her, but she would not change her mind. Sadly he went to the Sultan and said he would bring his daughter Scheherazade to him the next evening.

This news astonished the Sultan. "Is this really your wish?"

"It is not my wish, Your Highness, but my daughter's."

This surprised the Sultan even more.

Early on the appointed day, Scheherazade spoke to her younger sister. "I have a favor to ask of you. Will you come with me when I go to the Sultan's palace?"

"How can you do such a thing?" her sister cried. "The Sultan is a cruel old man. You'll be thrown into a foul dungeon like the others!"

"Not if you will help me with my plan," said Scheherazade. "If I succeed, I will be safe and the women of the city will be freed from the Sultan's cruelty."

"What do you wish me to do? How can I be of any help?"

"In the evening, when we are brought to the Sultan's chamber, I will ask that you be allowed to attend me." And Scheherazade told her sister what she must say.

The younger sister said, "I will do what you ask."

That evening the sister accompanied Scheherazade to the Sultan's chamber. As she helped her older sister remove her face veil and garments, she said, "Dear sister, I beg one last favor from you. Will you tell me one of your delightful stories before we part?"

Scheherazade turned to the Sultan. "Will Your Highness permit me to grant this favor?"

He nodded and belched, for he had, as usual, eaten too heavily. "Yes, yes. Go ahead."

So Scheherazade began a story. She told it so skillfully that the Sultan became absorbed in the story in spite of himself. Then, as the night grew late, she broke off at the most exciting part of the tale. Yawning, she said, "I am too sleepy to remember what happens next. But I will think of it tomorrow and finish the tale tomorrow night if Your Highness wishes."

By this time the Sultan was very eager to hear the story's ending, so he agreed to this request.

The next evening, Scheherazade finished the tale and began another. Again she broke off before the end, pleading that she was too sleepy to remember the rest of the story.

"Very well, you may take your rest now," said the Sultan, quite disappointed. "Tomorrow you must try to remember the rest of the story. I want to know how it ends."

Scheherazade continued each evening in the same way. The nights of her storytelling stretched on and on and on to one thousand and one, while the townspeople rejoiced in the success of Scheherazade's efforts to save the young women of the city.

What happened to Scheherazade after the one thousand and one tales were told?

One storyteller would have us believe that at this point Scheherazade and the wicked Sultan fell in love and lived happily ever after. Another narrator tells us that Scheherazade, having born three babies during this period, cast herself at the Sultan's feet, begging for her life for the sake of her soon-to-be orphaned children. The Sultan, entranced by the discovery of three male heirs—which he apparently had not known about—at once became a reformed man. Repenting his earlier cruel treatment of the other maidens, he spared our heroine's life. Needless to say, in this version they also lived happily ever after.

Those readers who can accept that the clever, courageous Scheherazade ended her days in this fashion may choose either of the above endings to the tale. But, having been moved by Scheherazade's courage, having empathized with her revulsion and horror at the Sultan's cruelty, and having enjoyed her clever strategy to free the women of the city and to survive herself, many readers may well be disappointed with these meek and improbable endings.

Rather than force Scheherazade to change her admirable character, I would suggest another ending. Freed at this point by the Sultan's death (for I loyally believe Scheherazade could have produced another thousand tales if necessary), acclaimed by the grateful citizens of Samarkand, she did what any clever storyteller would do: using her earlier education provided by the best tutors, she of course wrote down for posterity a more polished version of her one thousand and one tales.

This telling of Scheherazade includes the editor's interpretations of other possible endings of the tale. It is based in part on **ANDREW LANG***'s tale in* The Arabian Nights Entertainments *(1898). However there are a great many translations and variations of the stories, which have been represented widely in film and television as well as in literature.*

SUGGESTED READING

Favilli, Elena, and Francesca Cavallo. 2016. *Good Night Stories for Rebel Girls*. San Francisco: Timbuktu Labs.

Gaiman, Neil. 2015. *The Sleeper and the Spindle*. New York: HarperCollins.

Goble, Paul. 1993. *The Girl Who Loved Wild Horses*. New York: Aladdin.

Hamilton, Virginia. 1995. *Her Stories: African American Folktales, Fairy Tales, and True Tales*. New York: Blue Sky Press.

Lansky, Bruce. 2002. *The Best of Girls to the Rescue: Girls Save the Day*. Minnetonka, MN: Meadowbrook Press.

Martin, Rafe, and David Shannon. 1998. *The Rough-Face Girl*. New York: PaperStar Books.

McGoon, Greg. 2015. *The Royal Heart*. Lakewood, CA: Pelekinesis Publishing Group.

Ragan, Kathleen. 2000. *Fearless Girls, Wise Women, and Beloved Sisters: Heroines in Folktales from around the World*. New York: W. W. Norton & Company.

Sand, George. 2014. *What Flowers Say: And Other Stories*. Translated by Holly Erskine Hirko. New York: The Feminist Press.

Schatz, Kate. 2016. *Rad Women Worldwide*. Berkeley, CA: Ten Speed Press.

Yolen, Jane. 1986. *Favorite Folktales from around the World*. New York: Pantheon Books.

———. 2000. *Not One Damsel in Distress: World Folktales for Strong Girls*. Boston: Houghton Mifflin Harcourt.

ACKNOWLEDGMENTS

Several thousand individual folktales were read in a search for neglected tales of resourceful and courageous heroines to retell. In addition to public libraries and university libraries, the Reference Collection of Children's Books at the Donnell Library in New York City and the Osborne and Lillian H. Smith Collections in Toronto were very useful in researching the folktales. I take this opportunity to express my thanks to the reference librarians in both Toronto and the New York area for their generous help in locating needed volumes.

ETHEL JOHNSTON PHELPS *(1914–1984) held a master's degree in medieval literature; she was coeditor of a Ricardian journal and published articles on fifteenth-century subjects. Originally from Long Island, her activities included acting, writing, and directing in radio drama and community theater. Three of her one-act plays have been produced.*

SUKI BOYNTON *is the senior graphic designer at the Feminist Press. She is a graduate of Connecticut College with a BA in art history and has a degree in graphic design from the Art Institute of Charleston, South Carolina. She currently lives in Queens.*

CAN'T GET ENOUGH OF THESE GREAT STORIES?

You'll love the rest of the Feminist Folktales series!
Collect all four volumes today.

Turn the page for an exciting chapter from *Sea Girl*!

SEA GIRL

FEMINIST FOLKTALES FROM AROUND THE WORLD | Vol. III

WILD GOOSE LAKE

Long ago in China, a young girl lived in a small village at the foot of Horse Ear Mountain. Her name was Sea Girl and she lived with her father, a hard-working farmer.

No rain had fallen for many months; the crops hung limp and brown, dying for want of water. It seemed there could be no harvest, and food was already scarce. So each day Sea Girl went up on Horse Ear Mountain and cut bamboo to make brooms to sell.

One day when Sea Girl had climbed higher on the mountain than ever before in her search for bamboo, she saw a large blue lake gleaming in the sun. The water of the lake was clear and still. Not a single fallen leaf marred its surface, for whenever a leaf fell from the trees surrounding the lake, a large wild goose flew down and carried it away. This was the Wild Goose Lake Sea Girl had heard the elders speak of in the village tales.

Sea Girl carried her bamboo home, thinking of the clear blue water of the lake and how badly the people needed water for their crops.

The next day she took her ax to cut bamboo and again climbed high in the mountain. She hoped she could make an outlet from Wild Goose Lake. The village harvest would be saved if the lake water trickled down the mountain in a gentle stream to the farms below.

She began to walk around the lake, following the narrow, sandy shore. But the lake was surrounded by jagged rocks, high cliffs, and dense forest. There seemed to be no place to make an outlet for a stream. Later in the day, she came upon a thick stone gate. Her ax was of no help, and although she used all her strength, the gate could not be moved.

Wearily she dropped her pile of bamboo cuttings and sat down next to the gate. All was still, and the lake was a mirror reflecting the dark green pines. A wild goose swooped high in the sky, then glided down to stand on the ground nearby.

"Sea Girl," said the Wild Goose, "you will need the Golden Key to open the gate."

Before she could ask where she could find the Golden Key, the wild goose spread her wings and soared away over the lake. Sea Girl noticed a small keyhole in the stone gate, but there was no key.

Sea Girl walked on along the shore of the lake, searching for the Golden Key. She came to a forest of cypress trees, and sitting on a cypress branch was a brilliant parrot of scarlet and green.

"Parrot," she called, "do you know where I can find the Golden Key that will open the stone gate?"

The parrot answered, "You must first find the third daughter of the Dragon King, for the Dragon King guards the Golden Key to Wild Goose Lake." With a quick whirring of wings the parrot flew off into the forest.

Sea Girl walked on, searching for the Dragon King's third daughter. In a pine grove close to the lake, she saw a peacock sitting on a low branch.

"Peacock, peacock," she called, "where can I find the Dragon King's third daughter?"

"The Dragon King's third daughter loves songs. If you sing the songs your village people sing, she will come forth from the lake." The peacock dropped a feather at her feet and flew away.

Sea Girl picked up the feather and began to sing. Her voice was clear, and as fresh as a lark's song. At first she sang about the snowflakes drifting on the mountains, but the Dragon King's third daughter did not appear. She sang of green reeds bending in the wind. Still the third daughter did not come; the lake lay clear and still. Then Sea Girl sang of pale blossoming flowers on the hills.

Near the shore the water broke into a glittering spray, and the third daughter came up out of the lake to stand before Sea Girl.

"Deep in the lake I heard your songs," she said. "They are so strange and beautiful that I could not resist them. My father does not allow us to meet humans, but I have come to you secretly. I, too, love songs, and your songs are finer than mine."

Sea Girl asked, "Are you the third daughter of the Dragon King?"

"Yes, I am Third Daughter. My father and his people guard Wild Goose Lake. Who are you? Why do you sing your songs here?"

"I am Sea Girl. I live in a village at the foot of Horse Ear Mountain, and I have come all this long way to find the Golden Key which opens the stone gate of the lake. The people in my village are hungry and need water to save their harvest."

Third Daughter hesitated, then she said, "I would like to help you. The Golden Key is kept in my father's treasure room, deep in a rock cave. Outside on the cliff a huge eagle guards it, and he would tear to pieces anyone who tried to enter." She pointed to a rock cliff a little distance off. On the cliff perched an eagle nodding in the sun.

Sea Girl asked, "Would your father give us the Golden Key?"

"He will not help humans," sighed Third Daughter. "That is why he had the stone gate made to keep in the lake water. You must wait until my father leaves his palace and goes off. Then perhaps we can lure the eagle away from the treasure room."

So Sea Girl made a bed of soft pine branches under the trees and Third Daughter brought her fresh fish to eat.

A few days later she said to Sea Girl, "My father has left his palace. Now is the time to search for the key, but I don't know how you will slip past the eagle."

"We will sing to him," said Sea Girl.

The two girls lightly and quietly moved closer

to where the eagle perched high on the rock cliff. Third Daughter pointed out the entrance to the cave below. Tall ferns and reeds hid the girls from sight, and they began to sing. Each took turns singing the loveliest and most enchanting songs they knew.

At first the eagle just peered around curiously. Then, drawn by the strange haunting sounds, he flew down from the cliff in search of the source. Third Daughter crept quietly farther and farther away, and the eagle followed the enchanting sound of her voice.

Sea Girl slipped into the treasure cave to search for the Golden Key. At first her eyes were dazzled, for the room was filled on all sides with gold, silver, and sparkling jewels. But Sea Girl did not touch the treasure. She searched only for the Golden Key.

Just as she was about to give up in despair, she saw a small, plain wooden box sitting on a shelf in the corner. Quickly she opened it and peered in. There lay the gleaming Golden Key!

Sea Girl took the key and returned to where Third Daughter waited. When the delicate soaring melody of song ceased, the eagle shook himself, spread his wings, and sailed back to his cliff.

Sea Girl and Third Daughter hastened back to

the stone gate. The Golden Key fitted perfectly into the keyhole, and the gate swung open. At once the water rushed out in a leaping cascade, down the mountainside to the village. In a very short time, all the canals and ditches of the farms were full and overflowing with water.

Third Daughter saw that the village would soon be flooded and she called out, "Sea Girl, Sea Girl, there is too much water. The crops will be washed away and lost!"

Sea Girl quickly threw in the piles of bamboo she had left earlier at the stone gate. But that slowed the water only a little. Then the two girls rolled boulders and large rocks into the stream until the water slowed down to a small, bubbling brook. Now they knew the village would always have a steady supply of water.

When the Dragon King returned and found the Golden Key was gone, he was very angry. He banished Third Daughter from the palace. But Third Daughter went to live very happily with Sea Girl, and they sang their songs together as they worked.

So beautiful were their songs that each year ever after, on the twenty-second day of the seventh moon, all the women of the surrounding villages came together to sing songs and celebrate the heroic deed of Sea Girl.

This version was adapted by the editor from a tale in Folktales of China *(1965), edited by* **WOLFRAM EBERHARD**. *The story comes from a minority group living in southwest China, the Yi tribes of Yunnan. However, the Dragon King is frequently found in Chinese tales, and the importance given to folk singing is typical of many groups in southern and western China.*

The Feminist Press is a nonprofit educational organization founded to amplify feminist voices. FP publishes classic and new writing from around the world, creates cutting-edge programs, and elevates silenced and marginalized voices in order to support personal transformation and social justice for all people.

See our complete list of books at
feministpress.org